The

And The C

Coff

by

Terry Towers

The Assassin And The Girl From The Coffee Shop

Cover by: Terry Towers

The material in this book is intended for ages 18+ it may contain adult subject matter including explicit sexual content, profanity, drug use and violence.

Chapter 1

While replacing the milk bag in the milk machine, Lily's heart filled with dread. She was one of the two women at the coffee shop working the overnight shift and from what she could gather from her co-worker, who was currently in a heated argument on the telephone with her husband, she may be the only one for the remainder of the night. It wouldn't have been so bad if the dining room were closed, the front doors locked and it was only the drive-thru window open, but that wasn't the case. Any lunatic could stroll on in.

The sound of sobbing came from the kitchen and Lily sighed.

"Fine, you son-of-a-bitch!" Her co-worker screamed into the phone between sobs before slamming the receiver down. Lily was tempted to go out back and into the kitchen to check on Angie, but what could she say? Was it any of her business? Really? Lily was fairly new at the coffee shop and was just getting to know Angie, so she simply didn't feel comfortable consoling her when she had no idea what was going on.

There was a rustling of clothing, which Lily knew to be the sound of Angie throwing on her jacket. *Damn it.*

Several minutes went by before Angie, who had already removed her headset, brown visor and hairnet emerged from the kitchen, her dark eyes swollen and puffy from crying.

Lily opened her mouth to say something, anything, but was at a loss so snapped it shut again and waited for her co-worker to tell her she was leaving.

"I've gotta go home," Angie raised a hand, as though to silence any rebuttal Lily may make. "But I'll be back; give me an hour, tops. I swear I won't be long."

Giving the middle-aged dark-haired woman a weak smile, Lily nodded. "Take all the time you need. I'll be fine." She took a deep breath in and exhaled. "Honest. I'll be fine. The baker will be here in a couple of hours. I'm sure I can handle the one or two cabbies that come though until then."

Angie strode over to Lily and pulled her into a quick embrace. "Oh, thank you Lily, I owe you one." She sniffed as she released the surprised Lily and rushed to the front door. "Less than an hour I promise," Angie yelled over her shoulder as she pushed open the door of the coffee shop and rushed out into the parking lot.

Lily watched through the plate glass window that spanned the front of the restaurant as Angie scurried across the parking lot heading towards her older model Ford Focus. As she watched Angie leave, she removed her visor and hairnet. If she was going to work alone then she'd be damned if she was going to keep that horrid visor on her head.

Once the visor and hairnet were off she shook out her long golden blonde silken hair, before resettling the headset atop her head. She then undid the restrictive top two buttons of her matching brown uniform shirt and breathed a sigh of relief; she might be alone but at least now she now felt comfortable.

Taking one more look into the parking lot to satisfy herself that there were no potential customers heading her way, she rushed to the kitchen, into the large walk-in cooler and grabbed several stacks of cream cheese so she could top up the supplies in the front breakfast counter, for the morning bagels.

With her stacks of cream cheese in her arms she scampered across the kitchen and back out to the front of the store. She made it to the breakfast counter just as a customer strolled in the front entrance.

Normally she'd have been annoyed at the disturbance considering she now had the work of two people to accomplish before morning by herself, but she took one look at the sexy man strolling across the dining room towards the front counter and decided to make an exception.

He was tall - perhaps six foot or so - with short close-cut brown hair, broad shoulders, and a lean torso. His eyes were a dark seductive shade of green and his features, hard and chiselled. If she had to wager a guess she'd say he was twenty-eight, close to ten years her senior. He was - without a doubt - the hottest man she'd ever seen and she found her pulse begin to race as she looked him over.

"Now what did you do to be stuck working the graveyard shift?" he asked as he approached the front counter and flashed a sinfully sexy smile at her.

Lily could feel her face flush slightly as she shrugged. "Just lucky I guess." Depositing the cream cheese on the breakfast counter she made her way over to the register, to take his order. "What can I get for you?"

He clucked his tongue against the roof of his mouth as his eyes surveyed the short menu.

Lily groaned inwardly, hot or not, she hated customers like him. She had work to do, and standing there waiting for him to decide all he wanted was a coffee was a waste of her time. She needed this job, so everything had to be perfect when the day shift arrived in the morning otherwise it was *her* ass they'd be after. They wouldn't give a rat's ass that Angie had abandoned her partway through the shift.

"I guess I'll just have a large coffee, black." He nodded, pleased with his selection and shifted his eyes to meet hers.

Lily felt a shiver run down her spine as his eyes locked onto hers which immediately ignited a pulsing between her legs. After the span of several beats she broke eye contact and set to work on his coffee as he leaned over, rested his elbows on the counter, laced his fingers in front of him and watched her intently.

"Have you worked here long?"

Setting the coffee pot back onto the burner she snapped the plastic cover onto the paper cup and passed it to him. "A couple of months."

Straightening up he reached into the front pocket of his jeans and pulled out a handful of change. As he sorted through the various coins, a quarter slipped from his fingers and he bent to retrieve it.

At the same moment that he bent over, something warm and fast whizzed by Lily's face, grazing her cheek and seconds later the glass door of the microwave behind her imploded.

Mouth agape, Lily jumped at the sound of the microwave's glass door shattering, not even paying any notice to the wound across her cheek. Her eyes whipped back to the front of the store to see a small hole in the glass, which was now cracked, but had yet to actually break.

"Get down!"

Everything seemed to happen so fast. Lily had no idea what was happening, but briefly glimpsed the customer as he leapt over the counter towards her with the grace and speed of a panther, and tackled her to the floor.

She grunted as she hit the ceramic floor - hard, with his large, heavy frame covering her tiny one. The sound of glass shattering came from the front of the store, followed by a light thumping sound as something embedded itself in the wall above the back counter.

"Come on!" The man was already off her and onto his feet, crouching behind the counter.

As her eyes focused on him, they immediately noticed the gun he now held in his hand. She gasped and attempted to stand to run.

"Holy fuck woman, do you want to die? Stay down and follow me," he ordered in a hushed, but firm tone.

Lily gulped down the lump which was rapidly forming in her throat and nodded. Her heart was racing so quickly, she could actually *feel* it throbbing within her chest.

Standing, the customer fired the pistol several times out into the parking lot, each shot felt like a major explosion in her ears leaving her head reeling from the unexpected sound. Reaching down, he grabbed her hand and pulled the dazed and confused Lily to her feet and into the back kitchen with him.

"Wh…what's going on?" Slightly disoriented, she started to walk towards the doorway which led to the front of the store, but he grasped her forearm tightly, jerking her back to him. He grabbed her by the shoulders and spun her around so she was facing him.

"We don't have much time, so you need to listen to me." His voice was eerily calm, as though whatever was going on was an everyday occurrence to him.

Lily nodded, but her eyes seemed to want to look back out into the dining room.

He gave her a light shake and she snapped her eyes back to meet his. "Do you have a car?"

Lily nodded. "It's out back. Why? What's…?"

"Good. Give me the keys. Hurry up."

She hesitated for a moment and then rushed over to her purse sitting on the small round plastic staff table. Digging into her black handbag, she produced the keys to her ancient Dodge Neon and deposited them into his outstretched hand.

He gave her a friendly smile, which just slightly helped calm her frazzled nerves. "Okay, you need to listen carefully."

Lily nodded.

"There are some very bad men out there and they're going to come in here after us, so we need to leave. Now!"

Lily shook her head and took a step back from him. "No, I can't leave. Who are you? What's going on?" So many questions were racing through her head that she was having a difficult time thinking clearly. Was she in shock? She gave her head a slight shake trying to clear the fuzziness.

"I'll explain later, come on." He gave her hand a tug, but she remained rooted to the spot.

"Are you a cop or something?" He certainly didn't *look* like a cop, but that didn't mean he wasn't one.

He ran a nervous hand through his dark hair, gave her a lopsided grin and nodded. "Or something. Come on." He gave her hand another tug, but again she remained where she was.

"What does that mean, *or something*?"

The man huffed and rolled his eyes at her. "Listen, maybe I didn't make myself clear a moment ago. We need to go now... if we don't then those bad men will come in here and kill you *and* me."

When she didn't respond. He shrugged. "Suit yourself." Dropping her hand from his he raced toward the back door his three quarter length black leather jacket flapping out behind him as he ran.

Panic overtook Lily. As scared as she was to go with the sexy stranger, she was even more terrified that he might be telling the truth. "Wait!" she cried out as she ran after him just as he was exiting through the back door.

By the time she was out into the cool night air, her customer was already at the Neon. Panic gripped her. "Wait!" she screamed to him, bursting into a sprint and heading for him and her little car.

His head snapped over to her direction, but then proceeded to unlock the car and hop in. She made it to the passenger side and was opening the door as the car roared to life.

"Hurry." he urged, shifting the car into gear.

She slipped in and hadn't even gotten the door shut behind her when the car tires squealed and they sped out onto the road. The sudden forward jolt succeeded in shutting the door for her. She ran a shaky hand through her long hair as she watched the stranger from the corner of her eye weave her little car in and out of traffic as though he was a racing car driver and her Neon a Ferrari.

Why had she gotten into the car with him? She groaned inwardly. She didn't even know the man. For all she knew *he* was the bad guy. She'd just ask him to drive her home. Simple, right? She'd ask him nicely to take her home. Hell, she'd drop him off anywhere he wanted and just drive herself home, and then she'd have a much needed sleep and everything would make sense in the morning.

She took a couple of deep breaths in and released them slowly. Once she was certain her nerves had settled sufficiently for her to speak coherently, she focused her full attention on him.

"So is there someplace I can drop you off?"

He glanced at her out of the corner of his eye and shot her a grin. "Nah, that's okay. I have it under control."

What did he mean by that? She chewed at her lower lip for a moment before trying again. "Well, I think that I should be going home so I think that dropping you somewhere would be the best idea." When he didn't respond she added, "I won't tell anyone, not the police, not anyone. I promise."

He chuckled, turned his head and locked gazes with her, his forest green eyes on her sapphire blue ones. "You can't go home. Sorry."

Lily's frown deepened. "What? Why? I *have* to go home. I demand you take me home. This is my car, my rules."

His chuckling stopped and he shook his head. "Sorry. Can't happen. Not right now, anyway."

She tried to remain calm, but a bad feeling washed over her. Was she a hostage? Was he kidnapping her? She took another deep breath in then exhaled loudly. And even more importantly, why in *hell* was he so calm? If he could be believed and they were running for their lives; she would have thought he'd be showing a little bit of panic in his demeanour.

"Who are you?" It was a fair enough question as far as she was concerned; he could at least give her a straight answer on that.

Slowing the car, the customer turned off the highway and onto a road Lily was not familiar with, though considering how frazzled her nerves were and the fact that it was the middle of the night, she doubted she'd have known their location even if she'd been on that road dozens of times before.

"Oh, I'm so terribly sorry. That was so rude of me, just with being shot at and then escaping in a Dodge Neon, no offence, but not my first choice of a getaway vehicle…" When she huffed at him, he glanced over at her and shrugged with a slight smile touching his lips, "It slipped my mind." He extended his hand to her, while keeping his eyes glued to the two lane road they were traveling down. "I'm Scott."

When Lily hesitated in taking his offered hand, he took his eyes off the road long enough to read her nametag. "Ahhh, Lily. That's a beautiful name. My grandmother's name was Lily."

Her brow furrowed as she looked over at him in disbelief. Talk about a Jekyll and Hyde attitude change. *Maybe he's psychotic? Oh-my-God, that must be it and I'm stuck in a car with him!* She took his hand briefly and then snatched hers from his grip equally as quickly, though not quickly enough to avoid the warm sensation that flowed through her at his touch. She growled at herself for feeling attraction towards someone who was - quite possibly - mentally unstable.

"Well *Scott*, who are you *really*? And why were people shooting at you?"

Chapter 2

Scott took another glance at the young woman sitting in the passenger seat and sighed. It was unfortunate that she was being pulled into the madness of his life. It certainly wasn't his intention, but... as the saying goes, 'shit happens'.

What was he going to do with her? He had no idea. What did he *want* to do with her? He snickered at the thought; even in that hideous uniform she was a stunning woman. Her long blonde hair begged him to reach over and stroke it. Her bright blue eyes were the type that a man could lose himself looking into and her figure was nothing short of amazing; a nice little hourglass figure in compact form.

"Who are you really?" she pressed when Scott didn't respond straight away.

"I'm a freelancer," he shot her a smile that usually melted the ladies. To his dismay, it didn't with her. "Of sorts."

"Of sorts?" she raised a sceptical brow at him. "What kind of freelancer carries a gun and gets shot at in coffee shops?"

Damn. He didn't want to scare her by telling her the truth, but considering she might be with him for a while, he didn't see that he had much choice. "Well. I sort of..." Again, he shot her his patented Scott Redding 'guaranteed to make women melt' smile and again she seemed unimpressed. "I sort of... kill people for a living." When her mouth dropped open, he held his hand up signalling her to hear him out. "But only really *bad* people."

"You *kill* people?"

"*Bad* people. I kill *really bad* people." he felt the need to emphasise that point.

"So you work for the government?"

Scott couldn't control the bout of laughter that overtook him as Lily watched him in shock and disbelief. Once the amusement of her question wore off he shot her another smile. "Not for a few years. Fuck politics and fuck the politicians. Working for the government is so dishonest."

Lily's frown deepened and she shook her head. "You're kidding right? This has to be some sort of joke. This has to be. I want to go home, take me home, Scott!" Her eyes narrowed at him, "If that's even your *real* name."

He shot her an apologetic smile. "I'm sorry, I can't take you home."

She remained silent next to him, as he turned the car off the road they'd been traveling and onto an even more secluded gravel road. Thick forest lined both sides of the road and the only light was the dim glow of the car’s headlights.

The silence lasted all of five minutes before she started up again.

"Stop the car Scott. I want out! Stop the car," she demanded. Whatever fear and disbelief that had held her captive since the beginning of the fiasco seemed to lose its grip of her and be replaced by anger.

"I assure you Lily. This is for your own good. If you want to stay alive you're stuck with me."

She shook her head quickly, her blonde hair flying out around her. "No. No, I want out! I want out now."

He reached over and patted her knee, which she jerked out of his grasp as if his hand were on fire. "Look. I promise once we get where we're going I'll explain things a little better. You'll just have to trust me.'

"Where *are* we going?" She turned in her seat to face him fully, her blue eyes shooting daggers into his.

"Some place secure. I promise you'll be safe."

She huffed and settled herself back in the seat; her arms crossed over her chest and she stared out into the darkened forest ahead of them.

All things considered, she seemed to be taking things about as well as he could have expected. He hadn't expected Herrera's men to have found him so fast. The men who'd tracked him to the coffee shop were good, a little too good for his comfort, which meant they weren't Herrera's usual goons. He'd hired assassins -assassins just like Scott. He muttered a curse under his breath at the realization.

It was close to an hour since they left the coffee shop and he would have bet that by now, they'd discovered who it was that was working that night and had already ransacked her home and left a man or two there keeping watch over the place - just in case. Yes, there was no way he could let her leave him now, not in good conscience.

****

When he stops the car, I can make a run for it! Looking around her, the darkened forest looked menacing. *Make a run for it and go where?* She sighed. She'd end up getting herself lost in the wilderness, and mauled by a bear, or worse. Lily snuck a look over at Scott, who seemed to be content with not speaking for the moment. A freelance killer? So what he was telling her was that he was a hit man?

She frowned. Wasn't it the hit men who did the killing, not the ones doing the running? Perhaps she'd watched too many spy movies in her lifetime, it's not like she had ever met an actual killer before. Which led her to the question of what in the hell had he done to make himself a mark? An even more important question followed. Did she really want to be with him when they caught up with him again?

"Where are we going?"

Scott made a left turn onto a dirt road that she hadn't even seen until they were on it. After traveling for close to ten more minutes, he finally began to slow the car. "We're here," he announced as they came up to a small cabin nestled deep in the woods.

"Whose place is this?"

Scott waved a dismissive hand at her. "Home. Like I said before, it's safe."

Her eyes narrowed as she watched him slide from the driver's seat and slam the door shut behind him. With a heavy sigh, she grabbed her purse, which she was grateful she'd had enough sense to snatch as they rushed from the restaurant, and followed suit.

She found herself amazed at how quiet it was outside, aside from the rustling of leaves and the faint sounds of crickets chirping somewhere out in the night.

She turned her attention to Scott and watched as he strode up to the front door, removed his jacket, covered his fist with it and smashed out the lower pane of the door window. *What in the hell?*

"Why did you just break out the window, Scott?"

He carefully removed the remaining shards of glass from the window pane, reached through the broken pane and unlocked the door from the inside. He glanced over at her looking unperturbed by her suspicious tone. "So we could get in."

Planting her fists on her hips she glared at him. "I thought you said *you* were the owner. If you are, then why are you breaking in?"

He pulled his hand from the window and opened the door wide. "If you must know I happen to have lost the key a few weeks ago." he motioned impatiently for her to enter. "Come on, and watch out for the glass on the floor."

She hesitated a moment, but a growl which she suspected was a bear pushed her body into action as she rushed past him and into the pitch black cabin.

"There's a generator out back, I'll turn in on and be right back." He spun around and hurried around the corner of the cabin.

What? Whoa. Hell no, he's not going to leave me alone here, not even for a minute! "Scott?"

The darkened cabin sent a chill of fear through Lily. Born and raised in the city, she had never had exposure to the 'great outdoors', had never been camping, or even spent a night away at a cabin like this one so the forest seemed monstrous and intimidating. She was tempted to chase after him, but another low growl sounded from somewhere in the forest causing her to rush back into the darkness of the cabin, firmly closing the door behind her.

A shot of relief rushed through Lily when the sound of the generator roared to life and a number of overhead lamps burst into life displaying the interior of the four room cabin for her. When the lights came on she found herself in the kitchen area, to her immediate right was the living room which was sparsely furnished with a futon and plain wooden coffee table.

Walking across the kitchen which had a wood stove, a sink, pantry and a small table with two chairs, she peered into the bathroom. Again, simple in nature with a toilet, and old style claw foot cast iron bathtub and large closet; no shower. The bedroom was located off the living room and again was simply furnished, with a bed, a dresser and an end table. The walls of all the rooms were varnished pine and the floors covered with short brown industrial type carpet. It was what she'd expect a hunting cabin to look like.

It was far from the Ritz, but she supposed considering they had no other place to go, it would have to do. For someone who might enjoy 'roughing it' she figured it could be considered quite a desirable little forest getaway.

"It's not much, I know."

Lily jumped and yelped at the sound of Scott's voice as he spoke close to her ear, so close that his breath tickled her neck and send a shiver running down her spine.

She spun around to face him and, as her eyes swept over the length of his body, she fully appreciated just how large his frame was in comparison to her. His shoulders were wide and powerful, his chest broad and torso lean. Her eyes dipped to his groin and she took notice of the crease his cock made in his jeans. She looked away hastily for fear he'd notice her eyeing his dick, though she couldn't stop the flush that she could feel coloring her cheeks. "I...um…It's great."

He cocked his head and his eyes lazily worked their way down and then back up the length of her body, causing her blush to deepen. When his eyes finally met hers she saw they held amusement in them. "How old are you? Nineteen, twenty perhaps?"

"Perhaps... So how old are you. Thirty? Thirty-five?"

Scott chuckled as he shrugged off his jacket and tossed it onto a plain wooden chair by the door. Under his jacket he wore a plain black t-shirt that stretched across his massive chest and faded blue jeans. Again, she couldn't help the tremor of desire rush through her looking at him, or the heat forming between her legs.

"It wasn't an insult, I was just curious." He touched a strand of her hair and let it run between his fingers. "Cheerleader in high school, I bet."

"Class bully I bet," she countered, half angry at the fact that at the age of twenty-one she looked the part of a teenager to him.

Scott laughed outright. "I just turned thirty, and no, actually I was the school nerd. Got stuffed into a locker more times than I can count to be honest."

His arm grazed her left breast, as he walked past her and into the kitchen. A small electric jolt shot through her and she growled at herself in response. *Damn him!* "I seriously doubt that," she replied, following him across the room.

Shrugging, Scott opened the cabinet above the single sink. "I was in the chess club and a D&D enthusiast. But believe what you want... doesn't matter either way to me." Pulling out the flour jar he removed the lid, reached in and pulled out a key. Setting the jar on the counter, he reached back into the overhead cabinet and grabbed a bottle of vodka, twisted the cover from it and took a deep swig.

He walked over to her and passed the bottle to her. "Here take a drink or two; it'll take the edge off."

Lily accepted the bottle and looked down at the vodka a little uncertain about whether - given the circumstances - drinking would be such a great idea. *Fuck it!* She shrugged and tipped the bottle up, taking a long swig. The liquid burned as it raced down her throat, making her cringe and choke slightly as Scott looked on with amusement in his green eyes.

Deciding that perhaps drinking straight vodka wasn't her 'thing', Lily set the bottle on the small two person kitchen table and watched as Scott strode over to a large square ‘home sweet home’ mat just inside the front door. He pulled it up, slipped his finger into a knot hole in one of the planks and gave it a yank. A trap door of roughly four square feet opened to reveal a metal safe. He inserted the key in the safe and gave the handle a jerk, opening it to reveal a large black duffle bag and a laptop.

"Do you know how to use a gun?" he asked, removing the laptop and then grabbing the handles of the bag and also pulling it up out of the hole.

Lily shook her head. When he looked up at her with an eyebrow arched she realized she hadn't actually spoken her answer. Clearing her throat she replied, "No. But I can't. I…"

Scott's expression softened as if it was finally hitting him how overwhelming the situation was for her, "I'm going to teach you." Unzipping the bag, he pulled out a pistol and a large, scary-looking gun, and placed them on the floor beside him, with some ammunition.

"But…"

"Not tonight, I'll teach you in the morning." Zipping the bag he tossed it, along with the numerous guns still remaining in it, back into the safe and closed up the hatch, placing the mat back where it had been. Gathering up the guns he nodded to the laptop, will you bring that over and put it on the coffee table for me.

"Ummm. Sure." She picked up the computer, feeling secretly relieved that he hadn't asked her to carry the guns and followed him into the living room where she placed it on the coffee table in front of him as he sat down on the futon.

Flipping open the laptop, he plugged it into the charge that was already inserted into the wall outlet and turned it on. While he waited for it to start up, he set to work inspecting and loading the guns he'd grabbed from his safe as Lily looked on in awe. The way he handled the guns, with such familiarity and ease, both frightened her and gave her a feeling of security.

"You need to learn how to handle a gun, just in case," he explained passing the pistol over to her, which she hesitated to take. "The safety is on. It's safe for you to handle."

Taking the gun from him, she examined it, turning it over in her hands, inspecting every nook and cranny. She examined the muzzle, taking note of the manufacturer's stamp.

"That is the gun I'll be giving you. It's a semi-automatic pistol." Scott watched her intently as she examined the gun.

After finishing her inspection of the firearm, she gingerly passed it back to him. "I couldn't kill anyone, Scott. It would be of no use to me even if I *did* know how to use it."

Scott reached over and patted her knee, but this time she didn't pull away from his touch. After everything that had transpired, she suddenly felt as though she needed the contact; the reassurance that whatever mess she'd wound up getting herself involved in wasn't going to last forever. She needed reassurance that the stranger sitting beside her would make things better.

She caught his eye; the cool indifference that had been in them so far had warmed slightly and there was an underlying hunger in them. All of the craziness of the night's events seemed to wash away as her eyes lowered to his lips, and she wondered what they would feel like against hers. How would his strong arms feel wrapped around her, drawing her body against his?

She unconsciously ran her tongue along her bottom lip, drawing his eyes to her soft lips. He leaned in slightly; she was certain he was going to attempt to kiss her and she suddenly wanted him to.

He leaned closer, and just as his lips were about to brush across hers, a beep sounded from the computer. Scott jumped back, cleared his throat and refocused his attention on the screen before him.

"While I'm doing this, you should run into the bathroom and put some peroxide on your cheek. It's just a surface wound, but you can't be too safe."

Lily touched her left cheek, and was surprised she'd forgotten about it. However, with his mentioning it, the area began to throb. Standing she made her way to the bathroom and closed the door behind her. She opened the medicine cabinet above the pedestal sink and found the peroxide and cotton balls. Closing the cabinet back up, she peered at herself in the mirror. The wound didn't look too bad, some blood, but it was more of a scrape than anything.

She gingerly cleaned the blood off her cheek easily enough with a cotton ball and peroxide, but what disturbed her most was how horrid she looked. She looked exhausted. Her hair, which usually shone, looked dull and her eyes had dark circles under them. "Damn, no wonder he didn't kiss me," she grumbled.

Tossing the bloody cotton ball in the waste basket beside the sink, she went into the kitchen and grabbed her hairbrush from her purse. The least she figured she could do was run a comb through her hair.

Once she was satisfied her hair was tangle free she tossed the brush back into her purse and strolled back into the kitchen just as Scott was shutting the computer down. Digging into her purse once more, she pulled out her mobile phone, but as suspected, there was no signal so she tossed it back into her bag. "Does your computer get an internet signal out here?" She'd doubted it, but could have sworn she'd seen his laptop hook up to a signal.

Leaning forward, his elbows on his knees he peered over at her. "Generally, no. We're off the grid, but my laptop is set up a little differently."

Set up a little differently? She chewed at her bottom lip as she eyed the computer and then moved her gaze back up to meet his. She was temped to press him about it, but she was frankly too tired and doubted he'd give her the details. Not that she'd understand the details anyhow, she never was one for wrapping her head around 'teckie' stuff.

"You'll find some old clothes of mine in the dresser if you want to change into something more comfortable. You can have the bed; I'll stay out here on the futon."

Lily sighed. She was exhausted, but she doubted she'd be able to sleep, though her body demanded she try. "Alright. Thank you, Scott."

Chapter 3

Scott grabbed a pillow and blanket from the bedroom closet, stripped down to his boxer briefs and laid on the futon in the living room. The curtains on the few windows of the cabin were thick, but he could already see the hint of morning peeping through. He wasn't in the least bit tired, but hoped to get at least a few minutes of sleep, before Lily awoke.

Part of the reason for his restlessness was due to the fact that, at any moment, the alarm he had set up around the perimeter of the cabin could be tripped by unwanted company - it wasn't likely, but it was possible. Now that 'professionals' were in the game, things just got a lot more dangerous. The other reason was because he couldn't get his mind off the young woman from the coffee shop.

All things considered she'd handled herself as well as anyone could expect, so he had to admire her for that. However, he'd heard her sniffling in the bedroom for some time before she fell asleep, which had made him long to go to her. He'd ached to cradle her in his arms and tell her everything was going to be okay.

He didn't even want to think about how hot she'd looked in the boxers and undershirt she'd grabbed from his dresser, he couldn't get the image of her out of his mind. The way the boxers hung low on her curvy hips and the way the shirt clung to her naked breasts, her nipples tight and straining against the cotton, it had given him one of the worst hard-ons of his life.

Once she was in the bedroom and snuggled under the blankets he had come back out to the futon and rubbed one off. It helped - slightly. Though knowing she was on the other side of the wall, combined with the fact he hadn't had sex in nearly three years, was like putting cocaine within reach of a drug addict.

Scott had just begun to nod off when her screams jarred him awake. Within seconds he was in the bedroom and at her side with the pistol in hand. Scanning the bedroom, he realized it was not an intruder, but a dream that had awoken her. He sat on the bed beside her trembling body and stroked her silken hair; the strands were as smooth as satin running through his fingertips.

"I... I'm scared." she admitted weakly, "What if they find us?" She looked up at him, with her big blue eyes teary and his heart ached for her. "Could I ask you a favor?"

Scott shrugged. "Sure."

"Will you stay with me?"

"But Lily... I…" He squirmed uncomfortably as his cock began to rise at the thought of lying next to her soft body and of having her generous breasts pressed against him.

"Please." She pulled back the covers and patted the empty space beside her on the double bed. "I'd feel safer if you were next to me."

His conscience reminded him of how dangerous the situation could be. He couldn't get involved with her in any way. Getting involved with her would mean he'd be linking her life to his and no woman deserved to be involved with him - at least not at this current point in his life.

But maybe she just needed comfort. Or maybe just sex. Nothing more, just a good fucking and a warm body to curl up to. His eyes caught hers and he knew instantly she wasn't the type of girl that you could just have sex with and not get emotionally attached to. Getting into bed with her, even with good intentions, was not a sensible idea.

Scott sighed loudly and ran a shaky hand through his short brown hair. Then again, how could he refuse her request after dragging her into his mess? "Alright." Setting the pistol on the night table he slid under the covers and settled on his back.

Lily immediately cuddled next to his side, placing her head on his shoulder, and draping a leg across his thighs. He closed his eyes and tried to calm the storm of sexual energy building within him, but she felt so soft and the lavender smell of her shampoo, mixed with the faint smell of coffee assaulted his nostrils. Coffee and lavender wasn't the best of combinations, but it seemed to work on her.

"Don't worry, I won't let anything happen to you." When she didn't respond, he hooked his index finger under her chin and tilted her eyes up to meet his. "I've kept you alive so far haven't I?" he teased, hoping to see a smile form on her full, pouty lips.

A soft chuckle came from her as she relaxed slightly against him. Her leg moved up on his thighs and he inhaled sharply as her thigh brushed against the base of his cock. Lily froze next to him. She had discovered his erection under his boxer briefs. It hadn't been noticeable because of the darkened room, but she noticed it now.

She turned in his arms, crossing her arms over his chest and looking deep into his eyes. Her eyes held his for a moment, before dropping to his lips. A quarter of an inch separated their lips, causing a craving within him to taste her.

He didn't have to wait long... To his surprise she lowered her lips to his, sending his body into a frenzy for her.

His first instinct was to grab hold of her and pull her up onto him, straddling his waist, but he restrained himself. But *damn,* it was a hard thing to do. Her lips parted in a soft sigh and he took it as an invitation to slip his tongue past her lips and teeth in exploration of her mouth.

She rubbed her body against his, her groin rubbing roughly against his hip. He longed to slip his hand down the front of her boxers, and see if she was even close to being as horny for him as he was for her, but instead he slipped his fingers into her long locks, fisting them and pulled her mouth down harder on his, deepening the kiss.

Lily ran her hand along the smooth contour of his chest and the muscles rippled under her feather light, teasing touch. A moan escaped her lips as she pulled hers away from his and began to place a line of sweet kisses and teasing flicks of her tongue down the side of his neck.

Scott gently pushed her back against the mattress, his hand sliding up under her shirt and cupping her breast. Her nipple tightened as his thumb grazed it and another soft moan escaped her.

Her back arched, at his touch and she gripped tightly to his shoulders, urging his mouth to her breast.

Pushing the white cotton shirt up, he exposed her soft globes, with large pink nipples, begging to be sucked. He hesitated for a moment, catching her gaze and waiting to see if she was going to object. When he received no resistance, he captured the first already tight nipple in his mouth. His tongue circled and teased it, while his hand cupped and massaged the other rolling her nipple between his fingertips.

Her breasts were magnificent, and only increased his need to see and feel more of her silky ivory skin. He'd never felt skin so soft. As he continued his torment of her breasts, she moaned, and her hips began to rock. Letting her nipple slip from his lips, he grabbed the hem of the t-shirt pulling it up and over her head, and tossing it to the floor.

"Your skin is so soft," he groaned, as his eyes roamed her naked torso and chest. He lowered his mouth to her collarbone and kissed his way to the side of her neck. "And you smell so good." His cock was so hard it was beginning to ache with his need for her.

It was bad enough for him when he was out on the futon, thinking of her, but to actually touch and taste the flesh that had him hard for the past several hours, was nothing short of torture to him. "Tell me what you want, Lily," he groaned capturing her lips once more.

She didn't reply verbally, but her hand began to slowly move down his chest, over his rock hard abs and then, slipped under the waistband of his boxer briefs. He grunted, jerked his mouth from hers and stared down into her desire-filled eyes, as she grasped his cock in her dainty hand and began to stroke him, her thumb swiped over the head, spreading the pre-cum across the surface of it.

Following her lead, his hand slid down her stomach, under the waistband of her boxers, and palmed her bare mound. His finger slipped along her already soaked slit, longing for it to be his cock that was sliding between those soft, moist folds.

Lily moaned and bucked against his hand, as he slid two fingers deep into her core. She arched her back and closing her eyes, he watched the expression of pure pleasure settle on her features. Her soft hand continued stroking his cock in quick, fluid motions, and was bringing him to his breaking point way too quickly for his liking.

Sitting up, and reluctantly removing himself from her grasp, he hooked his thumbs in the waistband of her boxers, pulled them over her hips, down her legs and tossed them to the floor, exposing her bare pussy to him.

Lily's eyes opened, she propped herself up on her elbows and looked down at him, breasts jiggling slightly from her movements. She yelped when he slid from the bed, grabbed her legs, slipped them over his shoulders, and pulled her to the edge of the bed so her delicious pussy was fully exposed to him.

Beginning at her right knee, he began to trail feather-light kisses along her inner thigh, slowly, taking his time and enjoying the soft moans coming from her, which became louder and more frequent the closer he came to the apex between her legs.

"You're such a tease, Scott," she gasped when he reached his destination. Scott slipped two fingers between her folds and spread them wide, exposing her swollen clit and her pink pussy. The entrance looked so inviting, for a moment he struggled with the conflict of deciding which he wanted more, to taste her and have her come in his mouth, or to feel that tight, juicy pussy gripping his cock.

He opted for the first option, hoping that he could calm himself down enough so that when he took her, he didn't squirt his load within a couple of minutes. Lowering his mouth to her clit he flicked his tongue across it, and then smiled as she whimpered and thrust her hips up against his mouth, demanding more.

He lowered his mouth to her clit a second time, his tongue circling the swollen nub, before wrapping his lips around it and sucking gently. As his lips and tongue continued their torture of her clit, he dipped his fingers into her inviting pussy.

The taste of her pussy, the feel of her muscles clenching around his fingers, along with the soft noises that she was uttering were bringing him even closer to the brink than when her hand was pumping him. Lifting his eyes, he watched her body gyrate on the bed, her tiny fists gripping the sheets beneath her.

Scott removed his hand from her moist core and buried his face between her legs, his tongue probed her hole and she cried out his name. With a grin touching his lips, his tongue began its exploration of her pussy in earnest, thrusting in and out of her as though it was his cock. Taking pleasure at the noises coming from her, his free hand began to stroke himself.

As her arousal heightened, the pace of his tongue increased along with the speed in which he jerked his cock. He could feel her body growing closer. The soft trembling within her core told him she wouldn't last much longer, which was good since he knew he wouldn't be able to hold back for much longer himself.

"Oh God Scott. So close!" She bucked her hips, grinding her cunt against his mouth, and then slipped her fingers between her legs and began to pinch and roll her clit between her fingers as he tongue-fucked her.

His balls tightened and he could feel his body preparing to explode. Standing up, he replaced his tongue with his fingers, and began jerking his cock between her legs, intent on shooting his load on her mound and stomach.

Lily propped herself back on her elbows and captured his eyes with hers. Suddenly, she moaned, her body trembled, her pussy clenched around his fingers and then the sweet release. The evidence of her orgasm gushed over his fingers and hand.

"Oh dear God," Scott groaned as his shaft stiffened, throbbed and then exploded in a series of spurts, drenching her mound and stomach with his seed.

Panting hard, she collapsed back onto the mattress spread-eagled, with an exhausted sigh.

"I'll be right back." Giving her inner thighs a light kiss he left the room and hurried into the bathroom where he dampened a towel and returned to the bedroom with it. To his surprise, upon entering the bedroom, he was greeted with a series of light snores.

Chuckling to himself, he sank to his knees and very gently washed her stomach and between her legs, taking care not to wake her. Once done, he tossed the towel to the floor and carefully crawled into bed with her, pulling her body into his and cradling her sleeping frame in his arms, before placing a soft kiss on her temple.

She stirred, muttered something incoherent and then clung tightly to him, but didn't awaken. Within minutes of taking her into his arms, he also fell into a deep, contented sleep.

****

A smile touched Lily's lips as she slowly awoke. She'd had one of the oddest dreams... she was being shot at and then kidnapped and taken to a remote cabin in the woods, but *damn* the man in her dreams had been hot. She could actually feel the heat between her legs gather just thinking about him. What a wonderfully, erotic dream...

Lazily opening her eyes, she stretched out, in a cat-like motion. And then it hit her. She wasn't in her bedroom. She sat up with a start, now fully awake and took in her surroundings. She was in a small bedroom, with wood panel walls, devoid of any pictures or artwork.

It was the bedroom from her dreams.

"It couldn't have been real. There's no way," she muttered to herself, sliding out of bed, snatching up the soft brown throw blanket from the foot of the bed and wrapping it around her. She padded barefoot out of the bedroom and into the living room. No one. She checked the kitchen and bathroom, and came up empty there as well.

Panic began to shoot through her. It had been real and she was alone. *Oh my God! Did he leave me?* She rushed to the front door and threw it open rushing out onto the porch. She let out a sigh of relief as she peered out and saw her car still parked where they'd left it the night before.

Where was the man from the coffee shop? The man that... *oh-my-god!* She blushed, when the thought of what she'd done with a complete stranger came to mind. She turned and started to make her way back into the cabin in search of some clothing.

"I didn't think you'd ever wake up."

With a yelp, she jumped at the sound of the seductive male voice behind her. Spinning around she came face to face with the man from the coffee shop, the man who could do amazing things with his tongue. A sudden dampness began to gather between her legs.

"Oh God," she groaned.

Her eyes travelled the length of him, from his work boots, to his torn blue jeans to the black t-shirt which stretched across his muscular chest and shoulders. By the time her eyes made it to his, there was an amused grin on his handsomely chiselled features. His eyes shone with amusement and.... hunger... for her.

Oh, God! She looked down at herself and once more became very aware of her near naked body. The blush that was starting to fade, rose again, making her cheeks hot and, she guessed, turning them bright crimson.

"You know... about last night. I don't usually..." Gripping tight to the blanket with one hand she ran her other shakily though her blonde, dishevelled hair.

Adjusting the firewood that he had gathered in his arms, he nodded, the amusement growing in his green eyes. "I get it. You were scared."

She nodded her agreement. "Yes. I needed comfort."

He stepped closer, climbing the stairs of the porch. "You'd just been shot at; it's a completely natural thing to want to seek out comfort sexually in times of high stress. I get that."

"Exactly..."

He brushed past her, his arm grazing her breasts as he walked by, and sending a shiver of arousal through her. Quickly she regained her composure and it occurred to her what he was suggesting.

"What? No." Lily frowned as she followed behind him into the kitchen.

"No?" he raised a questioning brow at her as he unloaded the firewood.

"No." She cocked her head at him, and gave him a stern look. "I did *not* seek out your comfort sexually."

Straightening up after unloading the last of the logs he wiped his hands on his jeans and looked up into her eyes. "Well, *you* called me into the bedroom. And *you* were the one to kiss me."

Lily huffed. "I did not"

Crossing his thick arms over his chest, he stood waiting for the events of the previous night to clink into place for her.

A hand went flying to her mouth as her jaw dropped open. She almost lost hold of the blanket. "Oh my. I *did* seduce you."

Chuckling, he walked over to her and planted a kiss on her forehead, before giving her a swat on the rear and heading back towards the still open door. "I wouldn't say you seduced me," he called over his shoulder to her.

Spinning around, she watched as he strolled away. *Damn, his ass looks good in those jeans.*

He stopped at the doorway and turned to give her a wink. "In order to seduce me, I would have had to have been reluctant." His eyes slowly swept up and down the length of her body pausing at her breasts and he gave her a smirk. "Trust me, I'm more than willing to do whatever you want... wherever and whenever you want to do it."

Lily opened her mouth to speak, but words failed her, not that it would have mattered anyhow, he had already disappeared out of the front door, she assumed to retrieve more firewood.

Nervy bugger, she growled to herself as she scampered back into the bedroom in search of clothing. She'd show him. She'd known many men like him over the years, egotistical, self-indulgent, alpha male types who thought that women should just fall to their feet for them. She'd show him she wasn't just some bimbo he could add to his list of conquests.

Chapter 4

Feeling Scott's hard, rigid chest against her back, his arms wrapped around her waist and his breath on the back of her neck was unbelievably distracting, but she'd be damned if she was going to let him know it. She tried to concentrate on his words and the target that he'd set up for her. It was a simple board, with a bull's-eye painted on it.

The cool metal of the pistol felt ominous to her, as he placed the gun in her hands. The day had seemed like some surreal dream that she hoped to wake up from. She wasn't a killer; she'd never even *seen* a gun up close until today. She was a hostess at a coffee shop; she served customers for minimum wage plus tips. She didn't know anything about guns and really didn't want to start learning now.

Trying to remain calm, she attempted to focus on his words.

"Keep it pointed down, angled towards the ground at all times unless firing, understand. And always keep a firm grip."

She nibbled at her lower lip and nodded, tightening her grip on the gun, and keeping her fingers clear of the trigger.

"Alright, now. What I…"

"I don't think I'm cut out for this," she interrupted. "I don't think I need to learn it either, I trust you."

Scott sighed loudly in her ear. "Look. We discussed this at lunch. These people are serious people. I doubt they'll find me again

- find us, before I find them, but there are never any guarantees. The fact is this; *if* they find us, we'll be dead before we know they're here."

Lily's heart stopped for a moment and she found herself having a hard time swallowing the lump forming in her throat. His words were so grim that whether he meant to or not, he was greatly increasing her nervousness and fear and she felt her hands begin to shake.

She was suddenly relieved to have the support of his body behind hers to lean back against. As much as she disliked his slightly arrogant attitude, she was grateful to be with him. He made her feel safe, even when telling her the grim truth about their situation.

Taking the gun from her hands and thrusting it into his holster, he spun her around in his arms. She placed her palms on his t-shirt clad chest and looked up into his serious green eyes.

"I need you to be able to defend yourself, just in case."

"But…"

Her protest was cut off as his mouth came crashing down on hers. She moaned, as she slipped her arms around his neck and pressed herself against him, her breasts crushing up against his massive wall of a chest. His hands gripped her bottom and he pulled her groin tight against his, the ridge of his cock pressing against her.

Memories of how he'd touched her the night before, and how he'd made her come so hard that it nearly brought tears to her eyes came crashing over her. As much as she kept trying to deny it, she wanted him. Wanted him despite his arrogant demeanour, shit, perhaps even *because* of it. He was so sure of himself, so in control, so calm. And in turn his calm, mellow attitude seemed to help sooth her frazzled nerves.

Lily ground her body up against his, sucking his lower lip into her mouth and nipping gently. Scott groaned and squeezed her ass, again pulling her tighter against the ridge of his thick, hard dick.

Suddenly he pulled away from her, spun her back around, her blonde hair whipping wildly around her head as she turned and he pulled her bottom tight against his groin.

He leaned back into her, his warm breath on her ear sending shivers down her spine and fuelling the throbbing between her legs. "Be a good girl and shoot the target for me and maybe we can continue with the fun stuff later, in the bedroom," he said, his voice deep and husky.

A low growl came from the back of her throat. She wasn't sure which she felt most: aroused by him or pissed because he thought so highly of himself as to offer himself as a 'reward' for a job well done. She decided on offended.

Lily huffed, "The only way you got to see me naked last night was because you got me drunk beforehand."

A deep throated chuckle was her only response to that.

Yeah, it sounded like bullshit to my ears as well, she admitted to herself.

"Alright, back to it." Bracing himself behind her, he removed the gun from its holster and placed it back in her hands.

She reluctantly accepted the gun and kept it pointed to the ground as he had previously instructed, grip tight and finger away from the trigger.

"When it goes off, it's going to be loud and it's going to be a little scary."

Lily nodded.

"Alright? Ready it to fire."

Lily nodded again, never taking her eyes off of the gleaming gun in her hands, she pumped a bullet into the chamber and turned the safety off. With his gentle guidance she lined the sights up, aiming for the dead center of the bulls-eye.

"Strengthen your stance, Lily."

Another chill ran through her. She wanted to tell him to back away, his closeness was distracting, but at the same time having him close made her feel secure and helped her confidence. So, she gritted her teeth and pushed back her body's cravings for him.

Readjusting her footing, she once again lined the pistol up to the target.

"Ready? And remember, this is very, very important. Whatever you do, don't close your eyes. You need to be able to see your target in order to hit it."

"Yes." She gulped down the nervousness rising up within her.

"Fire."

She took a deep breath in, exhaled loudly, and then squeezed the trigger. The sound was near deafening and her first instinct was to yelp and duck as the gun jerked in her hands, but his solid, unyielding body behind her and his hands over hers denied her that instinctive reaction.

Silence settled upon them for a moment and she was disheartened to see that she hadn't even hit the board with the bulls-eye on it.

The sound of Scott clearing his throat finally broke the silence after what felt like an endless minute and he clucked his tongue against the roof of his mouth. "You closed your eyes didn't you?"

Chewing at her bottom lip she nodded and turned her head to look up and behind her at him, her nervous eyes catching his amused ones. "Kinda..."

His stern expression suddenly turned soft and a slight smile tugged at the corner of his lips. In that instant the cool arrogance his eyes usually displayed seemed to wash away to reveal a kind, sweet man that she was certain only a rare few people ever got to see. The bad thing was that she almost preferred the egotistical version of Scott, because this softer side of him was one that she could find herself falling hard for.

Lily's mouth went dry and her eyes traveled down to his lips, which seemed to be tempting her, and then back up to meet his eyes once more.

"Well, let's try again. This time with your eyes open," he teased.

Laughing, Lily refocused on the target. "I have to keep my eyes open. Got it."

In more ways than one, she mused.

****

Scott looked up from the keyboard of his laptop and watched as Lily, who was sitting next to him crossed-legged on the futon, poured herself another glass of red wine. "You had better lay off that wine; I don't want to be accused of taking advantage of you while you're in a drunken stupor again."

Setting the bottle down on the coffee table Lily held back her laughter and settled for sticking her tongue out at him. Taking a sip from her wine, she set the glass on the table beside the bottle and directed her attention to watching him.

Clucking, Scott went back to whatever it was he was doing. Lily attempted to catch a glance at the screen while trying not to look like she was being nosey. Finally, she couldn't keep herself in the dark any longer. "What are you doing on that?"

Ignoring her for another couple of moments, Scott typed in a few more lines, signed off, and shut the laptop down. Sitting back he draped his arm along the back of the futon and fingered a lock of her hair.

The tug of his fingers running through her hair sent a shiver through her. Closing her eyes she sighed softly, giving herself a moment to bask in the feeling.

Once they had finished their target practice that morning and Scott had deemed her good enough to carry a pistol, they had gone on a stroll for a couple of hours through the woods, checking the perimeter and the high-tech security equipment he had guarding the cabin. It was amazing to her, the cabin and the area seemed so plain, so primitive, but as she soon found out, looks were deceptive.

As the day wore on, and they spent more time together, they discussed lots of trivial things, but despite them being trivial, it was enough that she'd finally found herself trusting him. However, he'd been skirting around many of the serious, important questions she had and she wanted to get to them tonight.

"So what's with the laptop? What are you doing?" she inquired a second time.

"Well, I was just contacting some people who know some people who are going to find out *exactly* who is behind the hit on me and once I verify who it is, I'll simply go to their location - wherever it may be - and kill them." He held his hands out, palms up. "And then it'll all be over."

Lily found herself speechless for a moment. He said it in such a disconnected tone, talking about killing someone as if it were just a chore to be taken care of, equivalent to taking out the trash or walking the dog. "Just like that?"

Scott clucked his tongue and gave her a wink. "Just like that."

"Well," she picked up her wine glass and took another sip. "Don't you feel bad about it? You know, killing people."

His eyes locked to hers and the tenderness, the kindness that he'd let filter into his gaze and into his demeanour a number of times during the day was gone now. His eyes were now cold and devoid of emotion. "I don't murder for the sake of murder. Someone doesn't just hand me five grand to go after someone in an alleyway because they caught the man cheating with his wife. My targets are bad men, very bad, powerful men. Men who need to be stopped and an assassination is the most…" he paused, taking a deep breath in and then releasing it, "*effective* way of stopping them. I don't do it because I want to do it... I do it because it needs to be done. It just so happens that there are people willing to pay a lot of money for something that should be done anyhow."

Lily took another longer drink of wine, as she processed the information. He gathered another lock of her hair, and once more watched as the golden strands fell from his fingers, and once again the intimate gesture sent a chill through her. "Do you ever get lonely?"

Scott frowned and released the remaining strands of hair from his fingertips. He stayed silent, redirecting his attention to the window on their left and staring out of it.

Sitting up on her knees, Lily crawled over to him, pausing just before she reached him. Her movement drew his attention back to her and his eyes locked onto hers. The hard exterior he usually kept up was gone and she saw the man beneath the layers of armor once more. She'd been relishing these rare moments all day. Lily pressed her palm to his chest feeling the steady beat of his heart under her fingertips.

She wanted to lower her lips to his, she wanted to open herself up and give herself completely to him, but if she did, what then? There was no fairytale ending with this man, she knew this. From the way he'd talked throughout the day, he figured they'd be able to leave the cabin in a day or two. So, what then?

Last night she had taken comfort in his body, used him to relieve her tension, but to kiss him this time; to feel his naked body against hers a second time would be the beginning of a bond they'd never have a chance to strengthen or discover where it led. Was she willing to take that risk? To risk beginning to care, when she knew he was only a few days' fling whom she'd never see again.

But the haunted look of loneliness and the longing in his eyes; it was so intense that it left her breathless. Swinging a leg over his thighs, she straddled his hips, settling herself over him. She pressed her forehead to his, and for a moment their breaths intermingled, their breathing synchronizing. The fire within her came to life and the intense need to have him in rushed through her body.

She touched his jaw - that was just starting to show signs of a day old beard - with her palm, and then traced his lower lip with her thumb, watching him intently. Moving her hand back down to his chest she lowered her lips to his. Her lips grazed his tenderly, before she nipped at his lower lip.

"Lily," he groaned, threading a hand into her hair, cupping the back of her head with his hand and urging her lips down harder onto his.

She moaned softly, as their kiss deepened and the passion between them rose. He slipped his tongue between her lips to explore her mouth, his tongue lashing and frolicking with hers.

His free hand gripped her rear and pulled her groin tight against his. Despite his jeans and her borrowed boxers, she could feel his shaft rapidly gaining length and girth between them. She wiggled her hips over him and was rewarded by a deep, feral growl coming from the back of his throat, as he flipped her to her back on the futon. His massive, muscular frame hovered over hers; a hand planted on either side of her head.

Scott caught her gaze for a moment and a bolt of electricity shot through her at the intensity of his hunger filled gaze. She grabbed at the front of his black sleeveless t-shirt and attempted to pull him down to her, but to her disappointment he refused to budge.

"Scott?"

He attempted to give her a reassuring smile, but failed miserably. "I can only give you the next day or two. That's all I can offer, Lily."

She nodded and swept her palm across his cheek. He caught her hand and kissed her palm, before releasing it. "I know. It's okay. I want this." Every part of her body wanted and needed him, even if it was only temporary.

The hunger in his gaze flared up once more as he lowered himself over her. The ridge of his hard cock, pressed against her groin and his lips captured her earlobe before beginning to work their way slowly down the side of her neck. She sighed and whimpered as his tongue and teeth teased the sensitive flesh.

Her hips pressed up against him, trying to relieve some of the building tension between her legs. But it wasn't working... all that it did was fuel the fire raging within her and her pussy which begged to be filled.

"Too much clothing," she gasped as his lips reached her collarbone.

Chuckling, he sat back on his heels, settled between her wide spread legs, grabbed the hem of his shirt and pulled it up over his head, tossing it to the floor. Lily's eyes took in the magnificent sight of his bare torso and chest. His abdominal muscles were tight and beautifully defined. She couldn't resist the urge to trace the contours of muscle with her fingertips.

"You're beautiful, Scott," she whispered.

He laughed, and his face flushed slightly, which warmed the heart she was guarding so tightly against him. How could this man be a killer? She couldn't believe it. Nothing about the gorgeous man peering down at her at that moment would lead her to believe it was possible. *For now*, she decided, *I'll allow myself to believe it's not the truth.*

"Isn't that supposed to be my line?" he asked arching an eyebrow at her.

Grinning, she shrugged. "Guess you'll just have to come up with a better one."

Scott huffed, as he yanked at his belt and pulled it open and then began to work on undoing the string of buttons down the fly of his jeans. "See that's the problem. I'm more of an actions speak louder than words type of guy."

Grinning wider, Lily sat up, wrapped her arms around his waist and placed a trail of feather light kisses across his stomach.

"Umm, how about doing that just a little lower," he suggested his tone husky.

She laughed outright and peered up at him. "Lower huh?"

Grabbing the hem of the t-shirt she'd borrowed from him, he pulled it up. She lifted her arms in the air to allow him to tug it up and over her head, exposing her plump, yet pert breasts to him.

"I really love how large and pink your nipples are," he murmured, bending down and sucking one into his mouth. It instantly began to harden and she gasped from the sudden jolt that rushed through her. When the first one was nice and tight, his mouth moved to the second. "Mmm, and they get so nice and tight for me." he pulled the second into his mouth, nipping and tugging lightly at it, while flicking it with his tongue.

Lily moaned, gripped tightly to his shoulders and arched her back, giving him easier access to her chest. The familiar and uncomfortable wetness began to increase between her legs. While he continued his torment of her breasts, she hooked her thumbs into the waistband of his jeans and yanked them down to his knees, along with his boxer briefs, exposing his hard as steel cock.

When her hand grasped his dick, Scott let her nipple fall from his mouth and straightened back up, with a low feral growl as he watched her, his green eyes dark, with a look of deep seated lust in them. A shiver ran down her spine under his piercing gaze as she once more began placing kisses along his stomach and inching her way to his dick.

By the time her mouth reached the thick head of his cock, it was covered with pre-cum. She flicked the tip with her tongue, then swirled her tongue along the underside of the head, flicking and licking until every drop of the salty cum was gone.

Scott groaned and slipped his hand into her hair, fisting the silken strands and urging her mouth to take him in deeper. Looking back up, she caught his gaze, which had been transfixed on the sight of her licking his cock. Not breaking eye contact, she grasped tighter to the base of his dick and took the head fully into her mouth, sucking hard, while her tongue circled the circumference.

"So good, Lily," he moaned, his hips swaying slightly, urging her to take more of him into her mouth.

She moaned, excited by his arousal and took him further in as far as she could handle, until the tip of his cock, touched the back of her throat. She began working her way up and down, the length of his thick, hard shaft, having to use her hand to be able to work the full length of him. As his excitement continued to rise, so did hers.

Her pussy felt unbearably empty and her hips began to rock, with hers pussy's plea for some type of attention. She increased the speed she sucked on him, and slipped a hand into the waistband of her boxers. She parted her soft, wet folds and slipped a couple of fingers between them, immediately finding and filling her wanton pussy with two fingers.

His fists tightened in her hair, as he began to thrust harder and faster, until it was no longer her sucking his cock, but him fucking her mouth. Moving her hand from his shaft, she slipped it down to his balls, massaging them as he pumped into her.

"You have no idea how good my dick looks fucking your mouth Lily."

She couldn't respond; his cock was so thick and pounding so hard into her mouth all she could do was moan around him. She increased the speed her fingers stroked herself, alternating between stroking her clit and diving deep into her canal.

Oh, God! A knot began forming in her stomach, the knot that told her that sweet release would soon be on its way. His pre-cum invaded her mouth, and she greedily swallowed it down, anxious to feel him squirt his entire load to the back of her throat.

"I'm going to come," he warned, giving her a chance release him before it was too late, but she didn't. Lily wanted to swallow down every drop of him.

She was also close, but knew she'd never make it before him, so slipped her hand from her shorts and gripped his ass in her hands, pulling him tighter into her mouth with every thrust.

"Oh, god!" He groaned, as his balls tightened and his cock pulsed. The anticipation was killing her. She needed him to come almost as much as he did. Several more thrusts and he groaned loudly as his cock exploded in her mouth, his cum shooting deep into the back of her throat. She swallowed it down as though it were the finest of wines, moaning along with him, sending sweet vibrations through his dick.

His grip in her hair tightened, almost to the point of hurting and then relaxed just as quickly. Grabbing her shoulders he pushed her backward onto the futon.

"You never came." He said more as a statement of fact than as a question.

She was shaking her head and gasping as he pulled her boxers down over her hips and dropped to his knees on the floor while his hands slipped her legs over his shoulders. She dropped her knees and spread her legs wide for him. Without another word, he spread the lips of her pussy and began to devour her, as though he were a starving man, and her juices were the last form of nourishment.

She cried out, her nails digging into his shoulders, her hips pushing up to meet his tongue as it thrust relentlessly into her heated core. His fingers exposed her swollen clit and began stroking it, stroking and rolling it between his fingertips. She'd never experienced anything so amazing, so sinfully divine in her life!

Last night his tongue had played and teased, but tonight he was on a quest. And as the ripples of pleasure washed over her in frequent and increasingly intense waves, she knew he was going to have her coming within minutes.

She moaned and whimpered, her body writhing under his expert mouth and fingers. She bucked harder against his mouth and then took her nipples between her fingertips, pinching hard enough that she screamed out. Her body was so tight, she knew she was going to explode within seconds.

"That's right, baby. Come for me," he murmured against her pussy.

His words were the final straw. She pinched her nipples tight, her body tensed up and then she screamed out his name as her pussy contracted and then released. A flood of her juices squirted into his mouth as she was overtaken by one of the most intense orgasms she'd ever experienced. She released her nipples and brought her hands to the back of his head, pressing his mouth and tongue tighter to her as she was hit by second surge of spasms.

Once the second bout subsided she released him and slumped back onto the futon, drained and panting hard.

"Damn that was good. Amazing." Scott said, wiping his mouth with the back of his hand. He leaned over her and kissed her hard. His lips tasted of her juices and caused her desire to flare up once more.

She didn't have a chance to reply. He slipped his arms under her legs and behind her back and hoisted her naked and still trembling body against his massive chest. Wrapping her arms around his neck, she sighed, pressed a kiss to his shoulder and then lay against him as he carried her into the bedroom.

Chapter 5

Lily snuggled up tight to Scott as he effortlessly carried her into the bedroom. He gently laid her on the bed and stretched out on his side next to her. She turned to her side facing him, one arm propping herself up, while she used the index finger of her other hand to trace the contours of muscle in his chest and shoulders. The muscles flexed and rippled as her feather-light touch traced over them.

Scott ran a finger over the curve of her hip, stopping at mid-thigh and then back up again. A soft sigh escaped her lips. She closed her eyes and pressed her forehead against his shoulder. The idea occurred to her that if they could just stay there, in the cabin, for the next several weeks that she'd be perfectly fine with that - it wasn't as though she had a job to go back to; she was certain that taking off and leaving the workplace unattended was grounds for dismissal.

However, considering the circumstances in which she'd left...

Bah, she didn't want to concern herself with those things now. In her real life - her boring life - she worked at a mediocre job, for a poor wage so she could afford a rundown apartment close to her mediocre job. It hadn't been twenty-four hours yet since Scott swept her into his crazy life, but her usual worries, seemed a distant memory.

His fingertips ran back down over her hips and to her thigh, and again she shivered and her pussy tingled. She attempted to push her desires to the back of her mind for now, since she still had questions for him.

She pulled back slightly and looked up. Her eyes immediately caught his as he gazed down adoringly at her. "Can I ask you something?"

Scott simply shrugged, but the calm - almost serene- expression on his face told her yes.

"How did get into.... umm... your line of work?"

Scott's hand stopped at her hip and slipped around to her rear, pulling her tight against him, his semi-hard dick resting between her legs and throwing fuel on the fire that was beginning to grow, yet again, within her pussy.

"I worked for the government." he replied, his voice husky. He placed a kiss on her shoulder. "They trained me to kill for them, and I'm good at it. I didn't ask questions, just did what I was told. One day I decided I was sick of being their puppet."

She tried to focus on his voice, but his hand was on the move again pushing her to her back, and then slipping to her inner thigh and slowly working its way to her wet pussy. She spread her legs for him, inviting his hand and fingers to play.

"And so you work on your own now?"

"Yes and no." His intense hunger-filled eyes kept locked to hers as his fingers reached the apex between her legs and began to stroke and tease her folds. "I work for a private organization which contracts work out to us... freelancers. They work as a middleman, of sorts."

"Reminds me of some sort of spy movie," she teased, and then gasped as he plunged two fingers deep into her. Moaning she closed her eyes as he began to stroke the inner wall of her pussy.

He chuckled and then nudged her legs wider as he settled between them and lowered his body over hers, keeping his weight from crushing her with one hand braced at the side of her head. "Not quite as glamorous I'm afraid."

Scott began to run the head of his dick along her folds, up and down from her anus to her clit. She squirmed and bucked against him, attempting to impale herself on his massive shaft. Scott caught her eyes again, the head of his cock resting at her entrance. Damn, she wanted him in her so badly her stomach was literally aching.

"Lily, I want to... my God you have no idea how badly, but I don't..."

Lily couldn't help but grin wickedly up at him. "I though spies and assassins were supposed to be prepared for all possible situations." She wiggled her hips, taking his cock into her just a portion of an inch.

His breath caught in his throat and he groaned. "Damn Lily." He returned her mischievous smile. "I've never had a woman here. And it's been three years since I last..." his voice trailed off.

Her mouth dropped open as she stared up at him. "Three years?" How was it possible? Three years?

A slight flush touched his face. "Like I said. Not as glamorous as one might think. I'm not in the best occupation to be getting *involved* with other people."

Slipping a hand behind his head she brought his lips down to hers. "Good thing I'm protected so we can break that drought of yours." Hell, for all she knew the men who'd shot at them less than a day ago could track them here tonight and kill them both, and so that last thing she wanted was to die without feeling that beautiful, thick shaft of his diving deep into her.

While she expected him to fuck her fast and hard - he didn't. Instead, he slowly inched himself into her. Slowly, teasing her, causing her to squirm under him and thrust her hips up in an attempt to impale herself fully.

"Scott please, you're killing me!" she groaned.

He chuckled then captured her lips with his as he gave one final thrust, sheathing himself to the balls and stretching her pussy to its limits.

"You have no idea how good it feels inside of you Lily," he groaned against her mouth.

Oh my God! Oh, she knew; did she ever know! His cock felt like heaven in her. She wrapped her legs around his waist and held tight, both wanting him to pound mercilessly into her and also wanting him to remained buried deep inside of her; nestled in her hot, wet pussy. He filled her so perfectly full that she could have sworn his cock was made just for her and only her.

After keeping himself buried for a half-minute, he slowly withdrew and thrust back in. For several thrusts his speed was slow, intimate and intense - *and* the most torturous couple of minutes of her life. Scott had her whole body feeling like an inferno of pent up sexual energy, urgently begging to be released.

Just when she didn't think she could take his sweet torment a second longer he sped up, instead of slow, teasing movements his thrusts became hard and fast, making her cry out each time he rammed himself into her - balls deep. She clung to him, her legs holding tighter around his waist and her nails digging into his back, leaving angry red gashes along the length of him.

"Oh God, yes. Fuck me hard!" She cried out between whimpers and moans.

Everything about him felt so good. The feel of his thick shaft slamming deep into her, the feel of her warm juices as they seeped from her core and down her ass and the feel of his lips and teeth against the sensitive flesh of her neck; it was all bringing her rapidly to the brink.

"You're making me come already, Scott," she gasped.

He pulled his lips from her neck and kissed her soundly, his tongue thrusting into her mouth. She moaned against his mouth. Close, so close. Moments away!

A sudden heat rushed through her body and exploded within her pussy, rocking her body with the power of a mind-numbing orgasm. As she cried out his name, her pussy gripped to his cock, enticing him to fill her.

"Oh fuck, Lily." He buried his face in her neck, thrusting several more times while she held tight to him, before he rammed his throbbing cock into her a final time, releasing a flood of his cum into her needy pussy. "My God!"

Lily was still basking in the aftermath of her own glorious orgasm when Scott slipped an arm around her lower back, held her tight and flipped to his back, taking her with him while keeping his exhausted cock buried deep inside of her.

Stretching out over him, the feel of their mixed juices filling and slowly seeping from her pussy, fanned her desire yet again despite her recent orgasm. She rocked her hips slowly, but was stopped immediately by two large, strong hands grasping her hips in their palms.

Moving her eyes up along his chest, she caught his eyes and he smiled warmly down at her. "Just... stay put for a minute or two." He reached up and tucked a loose strand of golden hair that had fallen into her face back behind her ear. "A few minutes and you can ride me for as long as your heart desires." He gave her a slightly embarrassed chuckle. "Just need a second to recuperate."

A soft teasing growl came from her, as she flattened herself against him and kissed her way up the side of his neck to his earlobe. Nipping at his lobe she felt his cock jump inside of her and she groaned. Damn, he knew how to torment her so wonderfully.

Sitting up on him she brought her hands to her breasts and began to caress them, tweaking her nipples as she looked down at him.

"Oh, now I think I'm really going to enjoy the halftime show." Grinning, Scott laced his fingers behind his head and his eyes slowly worked their way up and down the length of her.

His dick jumped a second time and she felt it beginning to slowly rise within her. It was taking all of her willpower not to move on him. Patience had never been her strong suit, especially when her desire was kicking into overdrive.

Slipping one hand from her breast, she parted the lips of her pussy and exposed to him her quivering clit. His eyes immediately jumped to her pussy and he lay under her, eyes transfixed on her hand as she began to stroke herself.

Lily closed her eyes, arched her back and increased the speed of her strokes. By the time he was at half-mast she was rapidly moving towards a second orgasm.

"Damn, you're sexy Lily. Stunning."

His words sounded vague as she found herself being swept up in the waves of pleasure rushing through her. She felt his hands grabbing her hips and then him press her down tight onto him as his cock became rock solid inside of her. She began moving her hips in circular motions, the head of his shaft sweeping across her g-spot with each rotation of her hips.

She was close; so excruciatingly close. She increased the speed of her movements, riding his cock frantically now, aching to get off. His hips started to buck up against her, making slight slapping sounds as their bodied slammed together.

Taking her breasts in her hands once more, she squeezed her nipples hard, rolling and pinching them adding a slight amount of pain to the pleasurable sensations his cock was giving her. Less than a minute later, her body was overtaken by tremors which started at her head and ended with a throbbing between her legs.

Lily released her nipples, leaned backwards on him, her hands braced on his thighs and bucked hard, almost violently over him. Her breasts - nipples pointed to the ceiling, jiggled with the forceful movements.

She was so close, in a suspended moment of intense pleasure and then she felt his fingers between her legs and pinching her clit. His touch threw her over the edge and she screamed out as she came, her nectar washing over his cock and pooling between their bodies.

Spent, she didn't protest when Scott, grabbed her waist and pulled her from his dick. She collapsed on her back, her eyes hooded and panting hard.

"You're not done yet, honey."

The sound of his husky, deep voice had her eyes springing open just as he flipped her to her stomach, grabbed her hips so her ass was in the air, and slammed his dick into her. She whimpered as his cock drove deeper into her than it had before.

He pounded into her with a vengeance, while his balls slapped against her pussy.

Oh god! She didn't know how much more she could handle. She fisted the blankets under her and groaned. She was tired and God help her, her need to come again was growing. How many orgasms had she had that day four, five, six? She'd lost count, and she wanted it again, she wanted the rush again.

"God yeah, fuck me Scott. Give it to me," she cried out.

Scott grunted his response, ploughing into her harder and faster. When his finger teased the rim of her ass, she yelped and tried to pull away, but he refused to let her. Using her own juices as a lubricant, he slid his finger part way into her back entrance and she groaned.

"Do you like that, baby?" he asked fucking both her ass and pussy now.

"Y…yes," she groaned. A thousand times yes! These new sets of sensations were bringing her rapidly to yet another orgasm.

"Such a pretty ass." he thrust his finger in fully now, pumping it in and out in time with his cock.

His words came to her in a haze as she found herself helpless in the surge of another orgasm. Just as her body was about to release, she felt his cock become even harder and then heard his loud groan, as he pulled his finger from her ass, grabbed tight to her hips and pulled her roughly back against him.

As his warm cum released into her throbbing pussy in several fast spurts, she found herself also in the throes of her own orgasm. "Oh God! Oh Scott!" she cried out releasing, mixing her fluids with his. He immediately pulled his cock from her and their fluids came rushing down her thighs and dripping to the blanket as she collapsed, totally spent onto the bed.

She was now officially exhausted.

He collapsed beside her, and dragged her limp body over to his. Pressing his lips to her forehead he kissed her gently. "I could get used to this," he whispered into her hair as she snuggled up to him, draping a leg across his.

Lily sighed and then looked up at him, her blue eyes capturing his contented green ones. "So could I." They were both silent for the span of several minutes, lost in their own respective thoughts as they looked deep into each other's eyes.

"You know, my cousin Jessie who used to work at the coffee shop is engaged to Senator Morrow, maybe we could..."

He cut her off with a kiss. "I know what you're thinking, but this is something I need to take care of on my own."

"But if we could..."

Scott let out a loud breath of air and peered up at the ceiling. "You know what the authorities do to people like me?"

Lily frowned and shook her head.

He raised his hand for her to see, palm facing her. "See anything unusual?"

She shook her head. It looked like an average hand to her.

"I have no prints."

Her frown deepened and she looked closer, the coming night was taking over the daylight, leaving only minimal light in the room to see so she had to grab his wrist and pull his hand to within a couple of inches of her eyes to see he had no fingerprints.

"Why?"

"I'm a ghost, Lily. I haven't been the man I was born for so many years that I don't know who that person is anymore." The lonely, haunted look was reflected in his eyes once more and her heart ached for him, but she said nothing only waited for him to continue, scared that if she interrupted it would break the magic of the moment. "You see, people like us - people with no identities - we get taken to places, bad places. And at these bad places men do things too horrible to people like me in an attempt to find out what we know. Things so horrible that you beg for death."

A cold chill ran through Lily and she clung tighter to him. She didn't want to imagine it. She didn't want to think about the bad places or the bad men. Or assassins, or killing. She just wanted to stay there, with him, wrapped in his protective embrace.

"So you understand why we can't involve the police or anyone else for that matter? I need to take care of this myself."

Lily nodded and buried her face in his neck for fear he might see the tears welling up in her eyes. It was going to be alright. She knew she had to keep telling herself that. Scott would make it all okay again, she had faith in that.

Chapter 6

Scott couldn't remember the last time he'd felt so 'normal', as he strolled through the woods walking hand in hand with Lily while they checked on the security system. He liked the feeling, the closeness to someone else, both physical and emotional. There were times when what he was becoming scared him. Emotionless. He could kill a man at point blank range and not flinch. That wasn't normal. He knew this and it terrified the shit out of him.

She'd asked him why he was always calm, even in the face of danger.

He'd told her that it was his training, but that was only partially it. Another part was the fact he had nothing to live for, other than the assignments he acquired and the money in his bank account. But then again what good was money if he had no one to share it with? There had been no real joy in his life, until now.

He sighed, as he looked down at her. She caught his eye and smiled, that sweet, serene smile that made his heart beat just a little bit faster.

Damn it. He barely knew Lily; he couldn't feel this way about her. He couldn't feel this way about anyone. He knew what his future held; men who did his job didn't have long life spans. Even if he wanted to try to establish a relationship with her, how could he leave her for months on end worrying if he'd ever come back to her?

"Scott?" Lily's voice jolted him from his thoughts and he gave her hand a light squeeze.

"What? Want a quickie against a tree?" he wiggled his eyebrows at her and got an elbow to the ribs as a reply.

"Hey," he pretended to rub his 'sore' ribs. "That almost hurt."

Her grin widened and she rolled her eyes at him. "Why do you *always* have to be *such* an ass?"

He gave her a mischievous smile and a wink. "Guess you just bring out the best in me, honey."

She huffed and turned her eyes away from him. "So you think I'm getting better, huh?"

His brows furrowed. "What?"

For the second time in five minutes she rolled her eyes at him. "My aim."

Laughing he gave her hand another light squeeze. "You're doing remarkably well. I'm officially impressed." Giving her a sly grin, he added, "It's surprising what you can do when you keep your eyes open."

"Jerk."

He chuckled in response. "Keep up the sauciness and I will be pinning you to a tree and fucking you senseless." His dick did a little dance in his jeans at the idea and he groaned inwardly.

She stopped suddenly, gave his hand a yank and pulled him back to her. Grabbing the front of his black t-shirt in her fist she backed up a couple of feet until her back was wedged between his hard body and a massive maple tree.

His cock immediately sprang to attention, realizing that she was about to bring to fruition what he'd been joking about minutes before. Caressing the satiny soft skin of her cheek with the back of his hand and tracing the length of the wound on her cheek, Scott lowered his lips to hers.

With a soft moan, she parted her lips, inviting his tongue in. He eagerly accepted the invitation, while undoing his pants and pulling out his cock. Pulling back from her, he grabbed her shoulders and twirled her around so her back was to him and pushed her up against the tree, her palms flat against the trunk.

She'd borrowed a pair of his jogging pants which hung off her. The only thing holding them up was the drawstring. He reached inside the front of her pants gave the string a tug and the pants slid down to her ankles.

His cock throbbed, begging him to thrust it hard up into her sweet, tight core.

"Are you wet for me Lily?" he asked, brushing her hair to one shoulder and then kissing and nipping his way down her neck to her collarbone.

Lily moaned. "I'm always wet for you," she gasped.

Oh, sweet lord! Scott, stepped between her legs and kicked her feet apart. "I want you to spread wide for me Lily," he growled in her ear.

She thrust her ass back against him, taunting him with her wet pussy and tight rear. "If you want it, take it," she challenged.

Reaching between her legs, he slipped two fingers between her pussy lips and groaned. So fucking wet. He brought his two fingers to her lips which she eagerly took into her mouth, sucking hard and licking her juices from them.

Watching her suck his fingers reminded him of how good her lips looked around his dick and he was suddenly torn. Did he want her on her knees in front of him, sucking him off, or did he want to fuck her against the tree? He slipped his fingers from her mouth and thrust them back into her tight pussy.

He pumped his fingers in and out rapidly, stroking her inner wall until she was bucking and moaning against him, begging for him to enter her. Removing his fingers from her, he grabbed his cock and pressed it against her tight entrance.

"How much do you want me fucking you Lily?"

"Please, give it to me. I *need* it." She bucked against his dick, trying to impale herself on his shaft.

That was all the encouragement he needed. With one fast, hard thrust he was up and into her, balls deep and groaning loudly. So tight. Her pretty pink pussy gripped him, begging him to fuck it. As much as he wanted to make her come and hear those soft little noises she made when she hit her climax, he needed to get off more. *I'll make it up to her later*, he promised himself as he jack-hammered into her from behind.

With one hand on the trunk of the tree over her head to brace him, and the other wrapped around her, pinching and rolling her clit between his fingers, he pounded hard into her, over and over. Her pussy was so tight and so wet it was the closest thing to heaven that he'd experienced in his life.

"So tight. Such a beautiful, tight pussy."

He was quickly cresting the summit. Too soon, for his liking, but oh *God* it felt too damned good. The soft noises she was making, the cool air tickling his balls and ass as he pumped into her, and the moist heat that begged him to come, it was simply too much.

"I have to come, but I don't want to come alone," he told her, nipping at the sensitive flesh of her neck.

His words seemed to be all that she needed. "Oh-my-God Scott!" she cried out as her body trembled against him, and her pussy quivered around his dick. The feeling of her pussy muscles contracting around his dick was the final straw. He thrust one last time, burying himself to the hilt into her and unloaded his cum, squirting it deep into her.

With a satisfied sigh, he collapsed against her body, taking care not to lean too heavily against her slighter frame and hurt her. He took in several deep breaths and released them, before kissing her shoulder tenderly.

Taking a step back, he crouched down, kissed her lower back, grabbed the waistband of her jogging pants and pulled them back up, tying them securely for her. Once done with her pants, he pulled his jeans back up and tucked himself away again.

When finished, he pulled her tightly into his arms, stroking her long golden hair. "I could get used to this." He told her for the second time.

Wrapping her arms around his neck, she clung tightly to him. "So could I."

Beep, beep beep.

A feeling of dread mixed with a shot of adrenaline rushed through him at the sound of the security beeper in his pocket going off, warning that the perimeter of the cabin had just been breached.

"What's that?" Lily pulled away from him looking around for the source of the beeping sound.

Oh, fuck me!

"We need to get back to the cabin now!" He grabbed her hand and began jogging back to the cabin, tugging her behind him.

"Wh...What? B…but why?" She asked as she fought to keep up with him.

"They're here."

"Here!"

"Yes, it's okay, we just have to hurry and I need you to do what I say without question." He let out a sigh of relief at the sight of the cabin. He'd get her safe then deal with the men coming for him. If they were coming by car - which he assumed they were - then he had not quite ten minutes before they arrived.

As they reached the front porch, he pulled the key to the hatch from his pocket as his other hand opened the front door and ushered her inside, closing the door behind them.

Grabbing the pistol from the holster under his left arm he passed it to her. "It's loaded; take it, just in case."

Her blue eyes were wide with fear and her mouth dropped, but she nodded her head in acknowledgement. She took the gun from him, ensured the safety was on, and thrust it under the waistband of her pants at her back, muzzle down.

Pulling the hatch open, he grabbed the handles of the duffle bag inside and pulled it out. He unzipped the bag, pulled out another pistol and put it into his holster. He then grabbed a third pistol and what Lily had learned was a sound suppresser. He attached the silencer to the pistol before setting the gun on the floor next to him. Grabbing the handles of the bag once more he thrust it into the hatch and closed it back up. Not bothering to lock it, he just slid the 'home sweet home' mat back into place.

"Come on." He grabbed her elbow, ushering her into the bathroom.

"What do you need me to do?" she had no idea what she was offering to 'help' with. She doubted that she could ever actually kill someone, but she found the words tumbling from her mouth anyhow.

He opened a narrow, six foot tall empty linen closet, pressed on the back wall of the cabinet and a trapdoor sprang open. "I need you to live." Grabbing her shoulders he thrust her into the closet. "Get to the back and don't come out. No matter what, do you understand?"

"What? No." She tried to break free from his grasp, but was too easily overpowered.

Scott cupped her chin in his hand and brought her eyes to his. "Listen to me. Do not come out, unless I tell you. *Do you understand?*"

She felt tears welling up, but choked them back down. "But…"

His green eyes narrowed at her and his jaw clenched. "If I have to knock you out cold to keep you safe, I will. Don't make it come to that, Lily."

She recoiled at the cold tone his voice had taken on, and knew immediately it wasn't a hollow threat. When she nodded, a soft smile touched his lips and he captured her lips with his in a kiss so intense she felt it through every nerve in her body.

"Trust your instincts Lily, and don't make a sound, not even to clear your throat." With those final words he gave her a shove into the narrow hole in the wall and closed the closet door on her, plunging her into complete darkness.

She could hear his movement in the bathroom and felt slightly relieved that she could at least hear him, if not see him. The little cubbyhole he'd thrown her into was small, just large enough to fit one person and as she touched her fingertips to the walls, she realized it had been plated in steel.

She leaned back against the wall behind her, pulled the pistol from her pants and held it tight to her chest. She allowed the tears to freely slide down her cheeks for the first time since the whole ordeal began. Several minutes, which felt like hours went by with not a sound coming from the cabin, finally she heard movement.

The footsteps were light, but she could hear them, just faintly in what she thought to be the kitchen. She wondered where Scott was, she hadn't heard him leave the bathroom, but he was so light on his feet it would have been hard for her to tell.

Silence again. It was so quiet that she could hear her own accelerated heartbeat in her ears.

She was just starting to lull herself into a false sense of security when a soft 'whoosh' sounded from the bathroom. She heard a couple of normal, loud shots and then a thud came from the kitchen. She gasped, and then put her hand to her mouth. Feeling for the safely on the gun, she found it and clicked it off. He'd told her to stay in the closet until he gave word, but she couldn't. What if he'd been hurt and was lying on the floor bleeding?

He told her to follow her instincts and her instinct was telling her to find out.

Holding the gun tightly in front of her, its muzzle pointed to the ground like he'd instructed her, she crept from the closet. Crouching low, to make herself less of a target, she slowly opened the closet and peeped out. The bathroom was vacant so she silently eased herself out from her hiding spot and crept to the doorway of the bathroom with her back planted tight against the wall.

Peeping out of the bathroom, her eyes immediately jumped to Scott, crouched over the body of a blonde man of average build. Something caught his attention then; a figure suddenly appeared in the doorway with a gun raised to Scott's head. Luckily, Scott was quick drawing his weapon and exchanging shots with the man.

A slight movement caught the corner of her eye as she watched them exchange shots, a figure in the window. Instinct took over, rushing from the bathroom she raised her gun to the head of the figure in the window and pulled the trigger, sending three rounds into the surprised man, who hadn't seen or expected her.

Chapter 7

Pain shot through Scott as his body took the assassin's bullet in the shoulder and he was thrown to the floor from the force of the impact. But the pain was the least of his worries. The two assassins in the living room were both dead. He'd gotten lucky and been able to pull off a kill shot to the second assassin. However, he had suffered from a shot to the shoulder in their exchange of bullets.

But Lily had defied him and was now standing in the middle of the kitchen, a prime target if there were any more men out there, though he doubted there were. He'd assumed there would be two, so the third had been a complete shock to him.

He glared at her as he struggled to his feet. "You could have been killed," he snarled. He wasn't in the mood to sugar coat the situation for her, or spare her feelings. She'd done a stupid and reckless thing and he intended to let he know just how stupid.

Her eyes widened as they landed on him, and then on his shoulder where the bullet was lodged. He looked down and saw that his t-shirt was beginning to color with his blood. He ignored the problem of his shoulder for the moment. "Stay here and stay down," he ordered.

"But…" her eyes stayed locked on his shoulder. "You're hurt, let me…" she took a step towards him but he raised his hand to her, palm up.

"Stay back and hide. Now!"

She visibly flinched at the hard, icy tone his voice had taken, but he didn't care.

Nodding, she complied, scurrying back into the bathroom like a scolded puppy.

Dammit to hell!

Knowing he needed to check on the status of the third man, he walked out of the front door and around the side of the building to where the man's body should be *if* she'd managed to kill him. As he turned the corner, Scott came face to face with the dying man, spread eagled on the forest floor, lying in a rapidly increasingly large pool of his own blood. Scott guessed it would take about ten minutes for the man to bleed out onto the forest floor and it would be ten of the worst minutes of his life.

Marching over to the man, he kicked the gun from the assassin's limp grip and placed a booted foot on his chest. He cringed when he saw the dying man's face. He knew him well, had worked with him on a couple of jobs in the past as a matter of fact.

Upon seeing Scott, the man's eyes took on a look of relief. "Kill me," he rasped, his words so faint Scott could barely make them out. "Kill me, please."

"How many of you are there?"

The man gurgled, presumably choking on his own blood, but managed to gasp out: “Three”. Scott nodded and aimed the gun to the man's forehead. "Good-bye, friend." With that he squeezed the trigger ending the man's suffering.

With the immediate threat averted the intense burning pain of his shoulder took precedence in his mind. He made his way back into the cabin, barely giving the two dead men, bleeding out onto the floor a second glance as he made his way to the bathroom. By the time he reached the doorway of the bathroom he found himself becoming a little unsteady on his feet and at that moment realized that his blood loss was more substantial than he'd anticipated.

He needed Lily.

Leaning his good shoulder against the door jamb, his gaze immediately landed on her petite body sitting on the floor, her legs tucked against her chin, her golden hair draped around her and her shoulders heaving in what he assumed to be silent sobs.

Hearing him enter the room, she looked up and pushed her hair from her eyes. Her blue eyes, now red and swollen from her tears looked up and caught his. "Scott. Oh my God! I thought you said it wasn't bad." She immediately sprang to her feet and rushed over to him.

"I didn't think it was," he admitted stumbling to the toilet and sitting on the cover. "Get the first aid kit from the bedroom, it's under the bed."

Nodding, she rushed from the bathroom. As he waited for her to return he managed – with some effort and lots of pain - to pull his shirt from his body so he could examine the wound. Moments later, she came rushing back falling to her knees on the floor and flipping open the lid.

"Alright before you do anything I need you to go get a bottle of whiskey from the kitchen."

She frowned, but instead of asking questions she did as he asked.

"Open it," he instructed as she came back with the bottle in hand. Again she nodded and removed the top, passing it to him. He took a long swig, the alcohol burned as it slid down his throat, but because of the pain in his shoulder, he barely noticed the whiskey. "Alright, I need you to go into the first aid kit and grab the tweezers."

She nodded; fell back down to her knees and searched the contents of the large white metal case until she came up with tweezers sealed in an airtight bag.

He nodded to his shoulder, "I'm going to need you to take those and remove the bullet with them."

Her mouth dropped and her face lost several shades of its color as she considered his request. He hated asking her, but he had no choice, there was no way it would have been possible for him to do it himself. "You're my only hope, Lily. Please."

"I can't... I... What if I hurt you?" Tears began to run anew down her cheeks.

Gritting his teeth against the pain he leaned over and cupped her cheek in his hand and then kissed her lightly. "I'll die if you don't, Lily." he admitted, sitting back up. He hated having to admit that, admit that he needed help. But there it was. He needed her more than he'd ever needed anyone in his life.

She took a few moments to gather her composure and then nodded her head. "Okay. What exactly do I need to do?"

He took another swig of his whiskey, explained what he needed from her and then sat back and waited for the additional pain to begin.

****

Lying naked under the blankets on her side, curled up in a ball, Lily waited for Scott to join her. He was 'taking care of' the bodies. How, she didn't want to know, she would have offered to help, but by the time she was finishing sewing up his shoulder, she felt emotionally drained. So, she stripped her bloody clothing off and slipped into bed. The very thought of the dead men in the kitchen and the man she'd killed outside made her literally sick to her stomach, so Scott had insisted she lie down while he did what had to be done.

After an hour or so of waiting she finally heard Scott re-enter the cabin and a wave of relief washed over her. All she wanted at that moment was to curl up into his arms and have him tell her everything was going to be alright, even if it was a lie.

She listened to the sounds of his movements throughout the various rooms for close to an hour before he finally came into the bedroom. He hesitated at the bed and she could feel his eyes on her back, before he slipped in beside her.

"I'm sorry I was so long, I had to takc a bath to..."

"I know." She didn't want to hear the remainder of what he was going to say. He had to take a bath to wash the other men's blood from his body. One of those men being the man *she'd* killed. As she lay there, waiting for him to return, the thought that she'd killed a man plagued her.

He wrapped his arms around her and she took comfort in the feel of his strong arms, hard body and musky scent of his body wash. "I killed a man, Scott."

He kissed her shoulder. "No, you didn't, I killed him."

She attempted to turn in his arms to face him, but he held her in place with her back to him. "But, I'm sure I did."

"No, you didn't. You barely scratched him." He chuckled softly. "You must have closed your eyes again. I took care of him when I went outside to see if you'd hit him. So don't worry, you had nothing to do with his death."

She wanted to believe him, but deep down she knew he was lying to her. She was responsible for the death of someone. Instead of arguing with him about it, she pretended to accept his explanation, hoping that, as time passed, maybe she'd be able to convince herself that it was true; that she'd just grazed him and that it was Scott who had actually caused his demise.

"I figure we have about a day before more men are sent after us. So I've made arrangements for you to be taken to a safe place."

Alarmed, Lily turned in his arms to face him. The day was surrendering to the night, so there was barely enough light filtering through the dark curtains on the single window of the room to see the outline of his features. "Just like that? You're leaving me with strangers?"

"They'll keep coming until I put a stop to the root of the problem, Lily."

"And then what?" She couldn't help the panic rushing through her. She knew that whatever was going on between them was a limited time deal, but now that the time had run out she was scared to go back to being alone, to being without him. Not only scared of being attacked, but she'd already grown to care for him and she knew he was feeling the same things for her.

"And then you live the life you were supposed to and hopefully the nightmare I've put you through these past few days will fade." He ran his fingers through her hair as he looked down at her. "If things were different, if I were a different man, a better man, then I'd do whatever it took to be with you."

Damn him, she could feel the tears threatening to spill out onto her cheeks. Damn him for making her feel that way. Damn him for making her care.

"What I wouldn't give to be able to take you on just an average, typical kind of date. Show up at your place with a bouquet of red roses, and take you to an overpriced restaurant where the waiters are snooty and the food pretentious."

She chewed at her bottom lip, if only things were different...

"I'm so sorry to have dragged you into this, Lily. You have no idea how sorry." He touched her face and caressed her cheek with his thumb. "So sorry," he whispered, kissing her forehead.

Not saying another word, she buried her face in his neck and held tight to him, pressing the length of her body in close against his and savouring the feel of him next to her. Part of her hoped he was right that she'd forget about everything that had happened as time went on, but the other part knew she would never be able to forget.

Chapter 8

Three Months Later

As Lily stepped out onto her front porch and picked up the morning newspaper she could feel their eyes on her. She didn't know who *they* were - the people that watched her - but she did know that they were associates of Scott's. She hadn't heard a word from Scott since the morning he'd put her into a car with a couple of strangers and sent her on her way.

The people Scott had entrusted her with had given her a key to a safety deposit box at the American National Bank, and told her the contents of the box were hers to do with as she pleased. When she arrived at the bank to receive the contents of the box, she was shocked to find half a million dollars in it.

With the money she bought herself a house, a small house in the suburbs and a brand new Ford Shelby Mustang. The mustang was her pride and joy. Instead of going back to work, she decided to go to college; she figured with the house bought and paid for, if she lived frugally, she could pay the tuition in full for the entirety of the program and live without having to work while she attended school.

Life *should* have been good now. But it wasn't.

Every night since leaving the cabin she'd had nightmares of killing the man she'd shot through the window. The vivid nightmares reminded her that it hadn't been Scott that killed that man - it had been her - regardless of what he'd told her. She knew it was self-defence, but that still didn't stop the guilt from welling up within her.

Opening up the newspaper she flipped to the world events portion to read the headlines. One caught her eye.

'Known Columbian drug lord assassinated in home'

She read the article while standing on the porch, and under the watchful eye of her 'protectors'. When she finished reading the article, her instincts told her that it was the man Scott had gone after, and by the looks of it, succeeded in killing. Scanning the tree line to the left and right of her she attempted to see some sign that someone was there watching her to give some back-up to the feeling she had in the pit of her stomach that she was not alone.

"Was this him?" She called out, knowing she must sound crazy to the neighbors but not caring. "He did it! It's over. Tell him I want to see him."

Nothing but the sounds of chirping birds responded.

Frustrated, she ran a hand through her hair and continued to try and catch a glimpse of whoever was lurking out there.

"Please, just come out. Talk to me. *Please*."

She waited, but still nothing.

Anger overtook her and she tossed the newspaper to the porch. "Fuck you all and *fuck him*! And you can tell him that!" she screamed out, with tears in her eyes and threatening to escape. She stormed back into the house and slammed the door behind her.

****

Eight Months Later

"I had a great time Andrew, thank you."

This was her third date with Andrew, the accountant. Andrew was the first man she'd accepted a date from since her time with Scott. He was a pretty decent catch; handsome, loyal, dependable, and as boring as hell. But she needed to get out and start dating since it was apparent to her now that Scott was never going to show up in her life again.

He'd told her she'd never see him again, and he had lived by his word. She no longer felt like she was being watched either; she hadn't had that feeling for a few weeks now. In an odd way, she missed the feeling. When her 'protectors' left, they took with them the hope that she might see him again.

Slipping his arms around her waist Andrew pulled her into a tight embrace and lowered his lips to hers. She went with it, wrapping her arms around his neck and attempting to lose herself in his kiss, but it was useless. She simply didn't feel the spark with him, no matter how hard she tried.

Pulling away from him, she gave him a soft smile. "Good night, Andrew."

He hesitated. Considering it was their third date, she imagined he expected her to invite him inside, perhaps for a nightcap, but that wasn't going to happen. At least not tonight.

"Good night, Lily, I'll call you." Giving her a curt nod, he turned and walked back to his car. After a quick wave, he slipped in, started it up and drove away.

Lily watched until she could no longer see his tail-lights, before turning to unlock the front door. As she slipped the key into the lock, she froze. The door was already unlocked. Her heart accelerated. Giving herself a moment to calm down, she opened her handbag, unzipped the side compartment and pulled out a pistol along with a suppresser. She attached the sound suppresser and turned off the safety.

She took in a deep breath and released it slowly, calming herself in the process. She'd known this day *could* happen and she was glad she was prepared. Whoever was in her house wouldn't take her without a fight.

As silently as possible, she opened the door and crept inside. She didn't turn on the light. Instead, she gave herself a moment for her eyes to adjust to the darkness. The only light in the house was from the moon and the streetlamp at the end of her driveway filtering in around the breaks in the curtains.

She slipped her feet from the heels she was wearing and crept into the kitchen, keeping her back firmly planted against the wall. When she was certain the kitchen was clear, she proceeded on into the living room. Peering in from around the corner she noticed a figure - male, judging from his frame - sitting in her armchair across the room.

"What are you doing with Andrew, Lily? He's not the guy for you."

The voice was unmistakable. She'd dreamed of him every night for the past eight months. Some dreams had been horrific, some sweet and sensual, but always of him. Her body sang out with joy at the thought of him being here, but her anger and resentment posed more immediate forces.

Flipping on the light, she stepped into the room and raised the gun to his chest while she took a good look at him. He was as devilishly handsome as ever, forest green eyes gleaming and his smile, sexy and seductive.

"It's me... Scott." he assured her rising from the chair, his hands spread out, palms facing her in surrender, slightly confused she was still holding a gun to his chest.

"Oh, I know it's you Scott. Why do you think I have the gun raised to your chest?" She took a few steps into the room and stopped halfway to him. "Stay where you are."

"I'm not here to hurt you, Lily, you must know that," his brow furrowed and a hurt look crossed his features. He took a couple of steps towards her and she fired, the bullet embedding itself in the wall to the left of his head.

"Holy fuck, Lily!" His mouth dropped open as he looked at the bullet hole.

"I told you not to move, Scott."

"You could have killed me!"

"Oh, if I wanted you dead you would be already. I've gotten quite good with a gun, Scott. You trained me well, and I rarely miss a day at the range." She shot off another round between his legs, the bullet planting itself in the bottom of the armchair behind him. She raised the gun back to his chest.

He raked a hand through his hair. "You're angry. I get that."

She strode towards him, until the barrel of the gun pressed into the navy button down shirt he was wearing. "Angry. Yeah, I'm a little angry."

"Can we talk?" His eyes looked down to the barrel of the gun pressed into his chest. "Without the gun."

With a sigh, she flipped the safety on and tucked it back into her handbag and then raised an eyebrow at him. "Better?"

Scott released his breath in a loud puff of and raked his fingers through his hair once more. "Much. Thank you."

"I noticed you called off the hounds a few weeks back."

"Yeah, it's over. You haven't needed them for some time now."

She tossed her handbag to the coffee table and crossed her arms over her chest. "Since the day you killed the drug lord?"

Scott let out a nervous laugh. "Yeah, since then." He glanced over to the sofa. "Can we sit down?"

The anger was subsiding, slightly. Damn it. She wanted to stay angry, but her curiosity about why he’d shown up today after eight months overrode her desire to be difficult. "Alright," she made her way to the sofa and plunked herself down in the center, tucking her legs under her, the knee length skirt of her white sundress fanning out around her.

He sat next to her, and draped his arm around the back of the sofa, inviting her to lean into him. Despite her wanting to fall into his arms, she refrained. She wanted answers and she wouldn't get them falling for him again.

"I'm out."

"You're out?" she raised a curious brow at him. "What do you mean by you’re out?"

"I gave it up. I walked away. I want to be normal."

Scott took her hands in his and she let him. When she looked into his eyes she saw the real man behind them, the vulnerable man, and it tugged at her heart. She saw his pain, his regret and his frustration.

"Do you have any idea how many times I stood on the doorstep and begged them to tell you I needed to see you? That I needed to talk to you, even just a phone call? Or at the very least assure me that you were alive. Do you have any idea how many times?"

He brought her hands to his lips and kissed her knuckles. "I do. I thought it was better to let you move on. So you'd be safe and could forget about the nightmare I put you through."

"But I couldn't," she interjected. "I even considered going to see a psychologist so I could vent, but what could I say? What could I tell them that wouldn't have me committed to a psychiatric hospital?"

His frown deepened. "I know." He hesitated a moment, but then pulled her gently to him, pulling her onto his lap.

Lily cuddled close to him. She wanted to be angry with him. She wanted to so badly, but she needed him. She needed his hard body holding her tight, and the spicy musk scent of his cologne and the security she felt with him being around.

"I've *needed* you Scott and you left me alone." She felt the tears welling up and fought them back.

He pulled her tighter and kissed the top of her head and then buried his face in her hair. "I'm a horrible man, Lily. I don't deserve you, but God help me I want you. I've done so many horrible things, things that a normal person would never consider, but I don't want to be that man anymore. Those few days with you made me want to be a better person, for you *and* for myself. I want to change and start a new life."

Lily, looked up at him, her eyes locking onto his as her hand stroked the side of his face. The whole situation was crazy, but she couldn't help the fact that she wanted and needed him as much as he needed her. "So what are you proposing? We start dating?"

A grin touched his lips for the first time and he held up a finger, signalling for her to sit tight. Leaning over the edge of the sofa he grabbed something from the floor. When he straightened back up he passed her a dozen red roses. "Well, it would be a start. I think I promised eight months ago that if it were a different place and a different time I'd give you roses and take you to some pompous, overpriced restaurant."

"With the snooty waiters." Lily laughed as she accepted the flowers. She brought the roses to her nose and inhaled, taking in the sweet scent, before placing them on the sofa next to her. A smile touched her lips. "So you think flowers and dinner will win me over?" she teased.

Scott chuckled, slid a hand to the nape of her neck and urged her lips down towards his. "Well a guy has to start somewhere, right?"

Lily gave in to him, grazing her lips across his and feeling the fire ignite within her at the touch of his lips against hers. The eight months seemed to melt away and she once more felt the passion for him every bit as strong as she'd felt it the last time they were together. Except this time, he was really hers. He wasn't leaving her with the possibility of never coming back. He was there to stay.

Normal? He'd said he wanted to be normal and have a normal life with her. She doubted they could ever be 'normal'. But to hell with it... as far as she was concerned normal was highly overrated anyhow.

The End

Soft & Hard Erotic Publishing

www.elixaeverett.com

Contact Information

Website: www.elixaeverett.com

Email: terry towers@hotmail.ca

Facebook: Terry Towers

Twitter: TerryTowersXXX

Works By Terry Towers

Available Now - Singles

Frat Party Partner Swap

Under the Officer's Command

Daddy's Special Christmas Gift

All For Daddy (Taboo Edition)

The Marine's Naughty Sister (Taboo Edition)

Little Virgin Sister's Webcam Show (Taboo Edition)

Doing Her For Dad (Taboo Edition)

Deceiving Him (The Billionaires' BDSM Sex Club)

Her Brother, Her Hero

Her 'What if' Guy (Pursued By The Billionaire)

The Inheritance: Anything He Craves

Available Now - Themed Singles

Taken By The Team (Humiliation And Gangbang Fantasies Fulfilled)

Taken By The Marines (Humiliation, Gangbang And Cuckold Fantasies Fulfilled)

The Cop And The Girl From The Coffee Shop

The Politician And The Girl From The Coffee Shop

The Assassin And The Girl From The Coffee Shop

The Bounty Hunter And The Girl From The Coffee Shop

The Firefighter And The Girl From The Coffee Shop

The CEO And The Girl From The Coffee Shop

The Porn Star And The Girl From The Coffee Shop

Available Now - Series

Hitching A Ride

Hitching A Ride 2: To Trust A Con

Conjugal Visits

Conjugal Visits 2: New Beginnings

Sibling Rivalry

Sibling Rivalry 2: Never Say Never

Sibling Rivalry 3: In It Together

Moan For Uncle

Moan For Uncle 2: Keeping It Secret

Moan For Uncle 3: No More Secrets

Moan For Uncle 4: Skeletons In The Closet

Moan For Uncle 5: Love Or Duty

Moan For Uncle 6: To Love And Honour

Available Now - Mirror Editions

(Please note Mirror Editions are mainstream non-PI editions of some of Terry's bestselling taboo works.)

Doing Her For The Boss (Rewrite of Doing Her For Dad)

The Marine's Naughty Sister (Rewrite of The Marine's Naughty Neighbour)

The Virgin's Webcam Show (rewrite of Little Virgin Sister's Webcam Show)

Seducing Blake (Rewrite of All For Daddy)

Now Available - Bundles

The Terry Towers' Taboo Collection Vol. 1

The Terry Towers' Taboo Collection Vol. 2

Naughty But Nice Mirror Edition Collection

The Moan For Uncle Bundle (Books 1-3)

The Sibling Rivalry Bundle (Books 1-3)

German Language Versions

Taken By The Team (Humiliation and Gangbang Fantasies Fulfilled)

Von der Mannschaft Durchgenommen (Erniedrigungs- und Gangbangfantasien erfüllt)

Taken By The Marines (Humiliation, Gangbang & Cuckold Fantasies Fulfilled)
Von den Marines durchgenommen (Erniedrigungs- und Gangbang- & Fremdgehfantasien erfüllt)

The Marine's Naughty Sister
Die unanständige Schwester des Marines

Moan For Uncle
Sehnsucht nach dem Onkel

Hitching A Ride: Sexy Anhalter (Anrüchiges einverständnis erotik)

Sibling Rivalry
Geschwister Rivalität

All For Daddy
Alles für Papa

Italian Language Versions

Taken By The Team (Humiliation and Gangbang Fantasies Fulfilled)
Abusata dal gruppo (Umiliazione e Fantasie di Gangbang Soddisfatte)

Moan For Uncle

Un gemito per lo zio

Her Brother, Her Hero

Suo fratello, il suo eroe

Spanish Language Versions

Taken By The Team (Humiliation and Gangbang Fantasies Fulfilled)

Abusada por el equipo (Humillación y fantasías de sexo realizadas en grupo)

Moan For Uncle

El deseo prohibido

French Language Versions

Taken By The Team (Humiliation and Gangbang Fantasies Fulfilled)

Prise Par L'équipe (Fantasmes Assouvis D'humiliation Et De Viol Collectif)

Coming Soon

Moan For Hubby (Moan For Uncle 7)

The Politician And The Girl From The Coffee Shop 2: All That Glitters

Works By Nikki Nexus

Available Now - Singles

Daddy Says: Ménage Sex Games

Santa's Brothel

The Confessional: The Naughty Nuns Series

The Fire Eater

Taken By The Team (Humiliation And Gangbang Fantasies Fulfilled)

Taken By The Marines (Humiliation, Gangbang And Cuckold Fantasies Fulfilled)

Available Now - Bundles

Naughty But Nice Mirror Edition Collection

Coming Soon

Taken By The Mob (Humiliation And Gangbang Fantasies Fulfilled)

German Language Versions

Daddy Says: Ménage Sex Games

Papa sagt:Jetzt ein flotter Dreier

Works By Adrian Athens

Available Now

The Welding Instructor

Melting Point

Coming Soon

Men For Sale

Works By Elixa Everett

Available Now - Singles

Escort With 1000 Faces

Lust, Love & Luck

I Conjure Thee (Enslaved To The Djinn)

Midnight Encounter - Seduced By A Vampire (Quickie)

Tag, The Vampire's Game

Erotic Flash: A Vampire's Seduction

Children Of The Vampire King (Non-erotic horror)

Available Now - Series

A Night At Club Vampire

A Night At Club Vampire 2: Nigel

Visions Of The Vampire Queen (Book 1 Of The Vampire Queen Series)

Available Now - Bundles

Vampire Whispers - (Bundle of 4 Erotic Vampire Stories)

Coming Soon

Return Of The Vampire Queen (Book 2 Of The Vampire Queen Series)

German Language Versions

Midnight Encounter - Seduced By A Vampire

Mitternächtliche Begegnung: Von einem Vampir verführt

Works By Angelique Ambers

Available Now - Singles

Forced Into Submission (Her Fantasy, His Pleasure)

German Language Versions

Forced Into Submission (Her Fantasy, His Pleasure)

Mit Gewalt unterworfen (Ihre Träume, sein Vergnügen)

Excerpt For

The Bounty Hunter
And The Girl From The
Coffee Shop

By

Terry Towers

Available Now

Chapter 1

Portland, Maine - Day 1

Lincoln had been watching Angelique Donovan - a twenty-eight year old bail jumper - for several days now from the cover of his black 1969 Chevy Impala SS. It wasn't the most inconspicuous car to be on a stakeout in, but it was as close to a partner as he ever got. He'd been given it by his father on his eighteenth birthday - fifteen years ago - just before both of his parents died in a head on collision with a drunk driver.

He had four sisters, though he rarely saw them; life happens like that sometimes and he'd grown to accept that. They all lived in various areas of the North East, while he'd moved to Denver eight years ago and never looked back. For the most part, the car was the closest thing to family that he had and considering he spent more time in it tracking down bail jumpers, than he did in his apartment, he considered the car his home.

The dark-haired beauty was a hard worker, he'd give her that much. She pulled in long shifts every day and of the past three days he'd watched her, two of the shifts had been doubles. Regardless of how many hours she worked, she always greeted each customer with a wide, friendly smile. If he allowed himself he could have easily been pulled in by that bright smile, and the friendly gleam in her lively blue eyes.

But he wouldn't allow himself, because this time next week he'd be handing her over in handcuffs to the authorities in Denver, Colorado, where she was to stand trial on a murder charge. He had wondered countless times over the past few days how such a sweet, pretty little thing like Angelique Donovan could murder anyone. But he'd been a bounty hunter for close to ten years and one thing he'd learned in his time capturing bail jumpers was that anyone is capable of committing a crime. And in many cases it was the people you least expected that committed the worst kinds.

Lincoln sighed. "Well, show-time," he grumbled, thrusting his pistol in his shoulder holster, stuffing a pair of handcuffs in the pocket of his black leather bomber jacket and opening the car door. Not bothering to lock the car, he strutted across the parking lot of the coffee house towards the front entrance, keeping his eyes locked on Angelique.

He wondered if she'd be the type to run when she discovered who he was and why he was there. Most were, but considering it was a public place with so many co-workers around, maybe he'd get lucky and she'd go quietly, maybe even without him having to cuff her.

A guy can only dream.

He opened the front door of the coffee shop for a couple of elderly ladies to exit. They looked up at him, soft smiles touching their lips and muttered their thanks. He gave them a curt nod of his head and slipped through the open door. Of the three girls working the front cashes, Angelique was the only one busy so he waited in line for her.

"I can help you over here, Sir," one of the available hostesses told him but he gave a slight shake of his head.

"Nah thanks, I'll wait for Angelique."

He heard one of the girl mutter 'typical' under her breath followed by, 'she gets all the hot ones.' Lincoln grinned to himself at being referred to as a 'hot one' and removed the mirrored sunglasses that covered his stormy grey eyes and gave the hostess that made the hot one comment a wink. She flushed and scurried away into the back kitchen causing his grin to widen.

The customer before him took his coffee from the counter when Angelique presented him with it and left. His turn. Stepping up to the counter, with his thumbs hooked into the front pockets of his jeans he waited for Angelique to acknowledge him.

"How can I help you?" Angelique looked up, her eyes shining, her smile friendly. She chewed at her lower lip as she waited for his response, drawing his eyes to her full, glossed lips.

His cock stirred in his jeans and he growled at himself for letting his mind become distracted; even if it was just long enough to admire her subtle beauty. Shit, even the dorky visor sitting atop her head looked adorable.

Fuck and double fuck.

He cleared his throat, pushing his attraction for her to the back of his mind. He had a job to do and eyeing her like a teenager with a hard-on wasn't going to get it done. He slipped his hand into the inside pocket of his jacket and pulled out his badge. "Well, Angelique... you could help by coming quietly with me."

He locked gazes with her and waited for it - waiting for the pieces of the puzzle to fall into place for her and for her to realize she'd been tracked down and that she was going to be taken back to Denver.

That's it honey, think it over....

Lincoln held his breath, and before his eyes the realization set in. Her eyes widened, her smile faded, and she took a couple of steps back from the cash register.

Oh come on, don't make me chase you.

But she was going to run; he could see it in her eyes, as they quickly surveyed the restaurant around her. It was the look a deer got when it sensed a hunter and was about to make a run for it. She took another step back.

"I... I th-think you have the wrong person."

Lincoln stuffed the badge back into his inner pocket and then slipped his hand into his outside jacket pocket to produce the handcuffs. "Don't make this harder than it has to be, Angelique."

She sighed. Frowning, her eyes showed a look of resignation. "Alright," she muttered, "I'll go with you."

Slipping the cuffs back into his pocket, Lincoln let out a sigh of relief. He took a step back from the counter and waited for her to come around the counter and allow him to escort her from the restaurant.

Head down, she slowly made her way around the counter, until she hit the door for the kitchen. And just like that she made a run for it, dashing into the kitchen.

"Fuck!" Lincoln growled leaping over the counter and beginning what he assumed would be a short, yet annoying pursuit.

As he entered the kitchen, he felt his feet slip out from under him. He reached out to steady himself on the stainless steel counter next to him, but it was too late. Within seconds he found himself on his back, lying on the greasy floor. He turned his head just in time to see her smirk at him, give a tiny wave and disappear out the back exit.

"Oh, that cocky little..." he bellowed as he pulled himself to his feet and continued his pursuit of her, bursting through the back and into the back lot of the coffee shop. His eyes did a quick scan and happened to see her race into an alley between two apartment buildings.

He broke into a full run chasing after her. He dodged cars as he crossed the busy street and ducked into the alley he'd seen her disappear into. The alley became a maze of dead ends and high fences, so he was certain as long as he followed where it led, he'd have her.

****

Damn, damn, damn.

Tears blurred Angelique's eyes as she sat, hidden at the back of a stinky dumpster. How did life get this bad for her? Just six months ago she had everything, a promising career as a journalist at a prestigious newspaper, a nice home and was soon to be married to a man she loved and admired, Nathan Winters. Then, in the blink of an eye Nathan was dead and *she* was the one going to trial for his murder.

Her breath caught in her throat as she heard the sound of footsteps beside the dumpster. Just as the footsteps began to move away, she heard a squeak and felt something run across her exposed ankle. She yelped, and covered her mouth to try and stifle the noise, but it was too late. The owner of the footsteps started back in her direction.

The footsteps came back to the dumpster, and the lid was flipped open to display the bounty hunter glaring down at her. In other circumstances she would have found him attractive, but as he stood staring down at her trembling body, all she could thing about was that this was the end of the line for her. She was going to trial and then to prison for a crime she didn't commit.

"It's over Angelique, come out." He extended his hand to her, but she cowered away from him, inching away until her back hit the cold steel back of the massive dumpster.

The blonde-haired man huffed and his eyes narrowed at her. "You can't be serious. You have *no* idea how pissed I'm going to be if I have to come in there after you."

It may have been over for her; she was caught, but she'd be damned if she was going to make it easy on him. She cocked her head to the side and gave him the same condescending smirk she'd given him when she'd seen him slip on the vegetable oil she'd intentionally spilled on the kitchen floor during her escape from the coffee shop. "Guess you're going to have to earn that bounty and come and get me."

His features darkened and anger flashed within his deep grey eyes. "Fine. Have it your way." A deep, growl-like noise came from him as he pulled himself up and into the dumpster.

Seeing one final chance to escape, she scrambled to her feet and leapt over the side as he jumped in. She tripped as she landed on the cement ground of the alleyway, skinning the palms of her hands, but she righted herself once more and lunged forward.

"For the love of fuck, Angelique!" he shouted after her followed by a grunt and thud as he jumped from the dumpster and continued his pursuit.

She had just begun to regain a small sliver of hope when she felt an arm wrap around her waist and an impact which felt like the force of a Mack truck slamming into her back, sending her tumbling to the ground. As Angelique landed, the wind was knocked from her as his weight came crashing down onto her. She was still trying to regain her breath when she felt his weight lift, and her wrists being grabbed roughly and cuffed behind her back.

"We could have just done this the easy way, Angelique and you could have saved me a lot of aggravation. Now you have me in a bad mood."

Angelique huffed. "Do you honestly think I care about your mood?"

"You should since you're stuck with me for the next week. I can be a really nice guy, Angelique, but I can just as easily be a major asshole. Ball's in your court."

Once her arms were secure, Lincoln stood, grabbed her arm and pulled her roughly to her feet. Still not wanting to admit defeat, even with her arms secure behind her back, she tried to jerk her arm from his grasp.

Grabbing her around the waist he pulled her rear tight against him. The fight in her was pretty much gone, but she couldn't resist bucking against him a couple more times. She gasped and she froze against him as she felt his cock begin to grow and press against her bottom.

"Oh-my-god," she gasped. "You're actually turned on by this? By chasing down a defenceless woman?"

Lincoln stepped back from her, grabbed her arm roughly and pulled her along as they made their way back out of the alleyway. "You were squirming that tight ass of yours against my dick as if you were a damned stripper after a buck; what did you expect?" he defended, refusing to meet her gaze, though as she watched his expression she saw a flush beginning to redden his face. A slight grin touched her lips as a plan began to formulate in her mind, not the best plan in the world, admittedly, but one nonetheless.

She allowed her eyes to wander up and down the length of him. He was at least six foot. She guessed close to 6 foot 2, short-cut blonde hair and deep grey eyes. His shoulders and chest were thick and powerful. He was attractive, no doubt about it, in a rugged sort of way. The kind of guy she'd easily be able to fall for - under different circumstances.

8022825R00063

Printed in Great Britain
by Amazon.co.uk, Ltd.,
Marston Gate.